THE
GREAT
DESERT
RACE

THE
GREAT
DESERT
RACE

By Betty Baker

MACMILLAN PUBLISHING CO., INC.
New York
COLLIER MACMILLAN PUBLISHERS
London

Macmillan Publishing Co., Inc.
866 Third Avenue, New York, N.Y. 10022
Collier Macmillan Canada, Ltd.
Printed in the United States of America

10 9 8 7 6 5 4 3 2 1

LIBRARY OF CONGRESS CATALOGING IN PUBLICATION DATA
Baker, Betty.   The great desert race.
SUMMARY: Driving a steam-powered car, two young women
compete in the two-day Great Mountain to Desert Race
at the turn of the century.
[1. Automobile racing—Fiction. 2. Automobiles,
Steam—Fiction] I. Title.
PZ7.B1693Gr [Fic] 80-16483 ISBN 0–02–708200–8

THE
GREAT
DESERT
RACE

Automobile dealers in our fair and fast growing community have long debated the comparative superiorities of their machines, a debate they will settle on April 17 when all five will compete in a grueling two-day race from San Julio to Phoenix....

San Julio GAZETTE, *April 2, 1908*

Ride the Howdy Special! Greet the racers from a private train! Fare includes a pit barbecue in Yuma, where the racers will overnight, and a seat on the finish line in Phoenix!

Advertisement, San Julio GAZETTE, *April 2, 1908*

ONE

"Of all the dumb, dull topics." Trudy lifted her skirt so it wouldn't drag in horse droppings as they crossed Main Street. The only thing she wanted to know about automobiles, steam or otherwise powered, was how to drive one. But her brother Quentin just laughed when she asked him to teach her.

"You write the report," she told Alberta. "You're the one who wants to spend her free time at the dealership."

"But my father owns the ABCO dealership," said Alberta. "If I wrote a report about steam automobiles, it wouldn't be scientifically objective."

"Neither would mine. My brother sells steam automobiles for your father, remember?"

Alberta grinned. "But everybody in San Julio knows what *your* father thinks about *my* father's automobiles, so it evens out."

After almost four months of hearing about steam-powered ABCOs ("Drive an ABCO—Easy as ABC") at breakfast and sometimes dinner, Trudy's father had let Quentin sell him one, the new five-passenger model with all desirable accessories. But Mr. Philpot didn't find driving it easy as ABC.

Every time he tried to start the ABCO, he had to send for Quentin or Mr. Cunningham's mechanician. Quentin said his father didn't follow instructions; Mr. Philpot blamed the ABCO. They argued about it at breakfast and sometimes dinner. The last two days (very mild ones for March) Mrs. Philpot had run about the dining room shutting windows so the neighbors couldn't hear. Trudy thought they probably heard anyway.

Alberta's father had been in San Francisco for two weeks, tending one of his other businesses. He'd returned just the evening before and met Trudy's father at the San Julio Businessmen's Club.

Trudy could imagine what her father had said to Mr. Cunningham. She'd been hearing it every day for over a week. And she was sure Mr. Cunningham had said a lot more than her father had reported at breakfast or written in the *Gazette*. She'd heard the two men arguing in the Philpot parlor for years over everything from Teddy Roosevelt as president to the number of chimneys on the Orndorf Hotel.

But according to Mr. Philpot, Bert Cunningham had stated that his steam-powered ABCO was as easy to drive as an electric automobile. Then another dealer had said a steamer wasn't any more useful than an electric, either, that nobody could drive one outside San Julio because they wouldn't find enough water to refill the boiler every fifty miles. San Julio was high enough in the southern California mountains to get snow, but there were few streams with water all year. And on both sides of the mountains was desert.

Mr. Cunningham had declared, "An ABCO can go just as far without a refill as any of your gasoline automobiles. Farther."

One boast had led to another, and two hours later the Great Mountain to Desert Automobile Race was being planned, too late for the next morning's *Gazette*, much to Mr. Philpot's annoyance. He'd had Mathias Jr., Trudy's oldest brother, put out an extra edition.

Mathias Jr. brought the first copies on his way home from the *Gazette* building. Quentin, who hadn't known about the race until Mr. Cunningham telephoned before breakfast, had hurried across the street to confer with his employer. Mathias Jr. sat down at Quentin's place. Bertha brought him a stack of flapjacks and a fresh pitcher of maple syrup.

When he asked for coffee, Mrs. Philpot said, "It will keep you awake."

He grinned. "How else will I get the rest of the way home?"

Bertha brought the coffeepot. Trudy held out her cup but Bertha swept past to the kitchen, ignoring Trudy's outstretched hand.

Mrs. Philpot stared down the table at her husband. "Was a special edition really necessary, Mathias?"

"It'll put this town on the map," said Mr. Philpot, meaning that the story would be carried by eastern newspapers. Nothing in the *Gazette* ever had been.

But Mathias Jr. said, "With all the endurance and

7

cross-country races they run back east, who's going to notice this one?"

After Trudy reached Madame Butashky's Academy for Progressive Young Ladies, she had to agree. Nobody at the Academy mentioned the race. That could have been because they hadn't yet seen the *Gazette*'s extra but the fathers of some of the other young ladies had been at the Businessmen's Club. If they'd mentioned the race at breakfast, their daughters hadn't been interested.

Even Alberta, whose father was going to drive an entry in the race, was more excited about the fur hat and muff he'd brought her from San Francisco. All the way to the Academy she'd worried about the mild weather and if they'd have another cold spell before summer. But she must have thought about the race some time during the day because, bicycling home, she came up with the notion that Trudy should write a report comparing steam and gasoline engines, which was really what the race was about.

"You can draw lots of diagrams," Alberta told her. "Miss Peterson likes diagrams."

Each of Miss Peterson's students had to write a report on the scientific subject of her choice. It was going to count as one third of the final grade. Trudy hated science and hadn't started her report. Alberta had hers half done. She was using the flowers she'd pressed the summer before.

Trudy knew their long bicycle rides into the country hadn't really been to collect flowers. Trudy's birthday was three months earlier than Alberta's and, though they'd begged and pleaded, Mrs. Philpot had refused to let them celebrate together midway between. Young ladies donned long skirts on their sixteenth birthdays, not six weeks after or six weeks before.

Alberta hadn't liked being seen in short skirts when Trudy was already wearing long ones. So after Trudy's birthday, Alberta had developed a passion for collecting wildflowers. She'd lost interest after her own birthday party, much to Trudy's disappointment. Trudy had liked bicycling around the countryside. She'd felt like a character from her brothers' old dime novels, though none of their adventures had been truly dangerous.

And Trudy knew the real reason Alberta was now suggesting a report on automobile motors. It meant they'd have to spend time at the ABCO dealership and Alberta was sweet on Fred Auklander, her father's mechanician.

Trudy blamed it on the scandalous novel they'd read, the one being passed around the Academy in a *Weigard's Botany* cover. Trudy hadn't dared take it home for fear her mother or Bertha would find it. She'd read it at Alberta's house with Alberta leaning over her shoulder to point out the good parts.

It was about a countess and an innocent young man and their two weeks of passion on a tiger-skin rug. The really instructive parts had been replaced by ***s, but there were plenty of amazing things left, such as the countess purring like a cat and undulating like a snake on the tiger-skin rug.

Trudy and Alberta could imitate a purr, but when

they tried undulating on an old quilt they looked silly instead of seductive. Trudy decided countesses must be jointed differently but Alberta said they just lacked the passion of perilous love. That's when she'd started looking for excuses to visit her father's dealership.

It wasn't easy. Mr. Cunningham had other businesses. He was seldom at the dealership, and now that San Julio had telephones, it was hard to think of a reason to deliver a message personally. Then there was Trudy's mother. She'd never consider a business that catered to men a proper place for young ladies. This, more than anything, kept Trudy arguing against writing about motors.

But the subject was a good one. Nobody else at the Academy was likely to think of it and she could probably make Alberta promise to draw the diagrams. And it would be an Expedition Into Unknown Territory, as the dime novels called it. While changing clothes, Trudy decided to let Alberta persuade her. After begging a piece of apple pie from Bertha, she telephoned Alberta and suggested a stroll downtown.

Alberta came prepared. All her long skirts were new but so was the shirtwaist she'd chosen. And she'd doused herself with Florida Water.

It annoyed Trudy to be second-guessed so she argued harder and longer than she'd planned, all the way to Main Street, across it and down the other side. She gave in at the door of the ABCO dealership.

"And you'll do the diagrams, honest Injun?" she repeated.

"Cross my heart." Alberta solemnly X-ed the left side of her new shirtwaist, then opened the door.

Quentin popped out of nowhere to give them an argument. Mr. Cunningham's glass-paneled office was empty. Fred Auklander sat on an ABCO running board reading *Cycle and Automobile Journal*. When he heard what they wanted, he put down the magazine and stood up.

"Can't refuse the boss's daughter," he told Quentin. "Come on. I can tell you all about motors."

Quentin stared at him. He was used to treating Alberta the way he did Trudy and he usually treated Trudy as if she were still six years old and pestering him to shoot marbles. Trudy swept past him, haughty as old Mrs. Baumgarten. All she lacked were the pince-nez and grown-up hair style.

Quentin's muttered "Wait till Mama finds out" only gave her a sense of adventure, especially since there wasn't much chance of Mrs. Philpot finding out. Quentin wouldn't tell. He was equally guilty for letting them in. Not that there was much to see, just four different ABCOs, one with the hood removed.

Trudy was curious to see the boiler, which some people said would explode like the one in the lumbermill. But the ABCO's boiler wasn't a tank. It was a neat stack of coiled pipes. And though there was a larger standpipe in the center, Fred told them, the boiler would spring a leak before it could explode. The burner to heat the water looked like the Bunsen burners in the Academy's science hall, only this one burned gasoline.

Alberta leaned forward, listening wide-eyed as Fred explained generators and fuel linkages. Quentin paced back and forth scowling.

Trudy wondered if she could blackmail him into

teaching her to drive an ABCO. Then their father wouldn't have to worry about starting his. After she drove him to the *Gazette* office, she could drive Alberta and herself to the Academy. She could see them rolling up the curved drive. That would put Suzanne Davenport's nose out of joint, her and her French bicycle.

Alberta elbowed Trudy in the ribs. "Come on."

"What?"

But Alberta was already hunkering down with Fred Auklander under the rear of an ABCO runabout.

"See?" said Fred. "It's geared direct to the rear axle."

"Amazing!" said Alberta. "Trudy, you have to see this. *For your report.*"

But her signals said she wanted Trudy to crawl under and crowd her close to Fred Auklander. "Inflammatory proximity," the scandalous novel called it. Trudy wondered how she'd explain grease on the back of her shirtwaist to her mother. But she bunched up her skirt, crouched down and duck-walked under the rear of the ABCO. In the small space, the reek of Florida Water overpowered the odor of grease and gasoline.

"You smell like Francine Decker's wedding," Trudy whispered. "All seventeen bridesmaids."

Alberta tried to hide her grin.

But neither toilet water nor inflammatory proximity seemed to have any effect on Fred Auklander. He went right on explaining. "No gearshift, no drive shaft, no flywheel. Just fifteen moving parts."

He sounded like Quentin trying to persuade their father to buy an ABCO. Trudy could almost mouth the words with him, she'd heard them so often at breakfast. She wondered if she should pretend to lose her balance and shove Alberta into the young mechanician. She couldn't always tell about Alberta.

In spite of an over-indulgent father (according to Trudy's mother) and only a housekeeper to look after her, Alberta was one of the least progressive of Madame Butashky's young ladies. She was even looking forward to wearing corsets! But sometimes, especially when her temper was up, she did surprising things, such as blacking George Doty's eye when they were thirteen.

While Trudy debated what to do, Quentin's brown trouser legs appeared beside the ABCO. One foot tapped. Coins jingled in his pocket. It made Trudy nervous, too. She started to worry about her mother. Her heart stopped when Quentin said, "Great God! Here comes Papa!"

Trudy and Alberta looked at each other. Mr. Philpot always sent for Fred or Quentin by the office boy or by telegram. To have it on record, he said. Trudy had never expected him to come in person.

Before she could think what to do, the back door banged open and Alberta's father stormed in. They'd have heard a gasoline engine when it entered the alley, but steamers were silent so they'd had no warning. And even indulgent Mr. Cunningham wouldn't like Alberta scrooching under automobiles with his mechanician.

If he noticed them, he gave no sign. He stomped past, muttering curses. Trudy had heard worse from her brothers. So had Alberta, but since she'd graduated to long skirts she'd become almost as concerned about proprieties as Trudy's mother. She started to act flustered and embarrassed but Fred had already backed out from under the runabout.

He walked toward the front and started to laugh.

"It is not funny," snapped Mr. Cunningham.

"No, sir," said Fred, but he kept on laughing.

Trudy and Alberta crept out for a look, stepping away from the ABCO so they could see out the windows. Trudy's father was driving his ABCO but with one of the carriage horses hitched to the front. Across the green sides were signs: THIS IS THE ONLY WAY AN ABCO CAN BE DRIVEN. He'd collected a small crowd of followers, and more people gathered on the sidewalk as he reined in the horse.

Alberta climbed into the runabout, either for a better view or so Fred would hand her up. Trudy stepped behind it, hoping her father wouldn't notice her skirts beneath the automobile. The bell on the door jangled and a gold cigar band blew against a tire on the red ABCO opposite.

Mr. Cunningham shouted, "That sign is a slanderous lie, Mathias! The ABCO is the easiest automobile in the world to drive! Except for an electric." His tone dismissed electrics as of no account.

"The easiest and *fastest*," he went on. "An *ABCO* is going to win that race you're touting in the Extra."

"Not if it won't start," said Trudy's father.

From the way the cigar band kept trying to escape, Trudy knew the door was still open. She wondered which of the men wanted an audience. Probably both, her father to have witnesses and Mr. Cunningham because he believed in advertising, though not the sort Mr. Philpot was giving him. She didn't have to look to know people were pushing through the open door.

Her father spoke as if he were on a platform address-ing a gathering. "You sold me this collection of steam pipes with a money-back guarantee, Bert. I expect you to honor it."

"I stand foursquare behind my guarantees. But *there is nothing wrong with that automobile!*"

"*It doesn't start!*"

Mr. Cunningham lowered his voice but he sounded under considerable strain. "Quentin and Fred don't have any trouble starting it. Do you, boys?"

Trudy's father didn't give them a chance to answer. "*I don't have half an hour to waste when I need to go some-where!*"

"*It only takes five minutes if you know what you're doing!*"

"I AM NOT A MECHANICIAN!"

"YOU DON'T NEED TO BE. ONLY A JACKASS COULDN'T DRIVE AN ABCO!"

There was a silence during which Trudy's father must have noticed Alberta sitting in the runabout. Trudy leaned against its back, trying not to move.

"What about your daughter?" said Mr. Philpot.

Trudy hadn't heard him sound so pleased since his newspaper had forced Councilman Very to resign.

Mr. Cunningham didn't hesitate. "No cranking, no clutch, no gears to shift. Of course she could drive an ABCO."

"In the race?"

If they'd been in the Philpot dining room or parlor, most likely Mr. Cunningham would have said, "Certainly!" and Trudy's father would have laughed at him and they'd have gone on to politics or the sad state of the economy. But they were at the dealership with the door open to an eager audience.

Somebody called, "Prove it, Bert. Let her drive in the race."

Another voice said, "That won't prove nothing. He'll send his mechanician to do the real driving."

The ABCO jounced against Trudy's back as Alberta moved. Trudy smothered a laugh. Poor Alberta, torn between inflammatory proximity in an automobile and the scandal of traveling alone with an unrelated man. Not that any respectable family would permit it.

"No, no," said Mr. Cunningham. "That wouldn't be proper, in more ways than one. No, if my daughter should drive in the race—and she could, easy as ABC—then Mr. Philpot's daughter would accompany her as mechanician."

Trudy gasped, then clapped a hand over her mouth. To drive an automobile! In a race!

Her father said, "Trudy doesn't know anything about automobiles."

He sounded alarmed, but Trudy didn't know if it was on her account or because now he was the one who'd have to back down.

Mr. Cunningham said, "She knows more than you do, Mathias. She's been studying them closely."

So he had seen them under the runabout.

"Well, Mathias?" he said.

There was a lot of encouragement from the audience. Trudy almost suffocated holding her breath until her father answered.

"They'd have to drive my ABCO," he said. "Otherwise it wouldn't prove your guarantee."

It also wouldn't be fair. The heavy touring model would have to race against light sportsters and runabouts. If Trudy's father was trying to give Mr. Cunningham an honorable way out, the crowd wasn't going to let him take it. There were more shouts and dares and, this time, a few remarks about courage. Whoever backed down would be the talk of San Julio. Mr. Cunningham had his business reputation to consider, and Trudy could almost hear her father wondering how big a story it would make.

So the decision teetered there like a bicycle on the crest of Harmon's Hill, needing just a touch on the pedal to get over the top. Trudy wasn't going to let it roll back down. She wanted to see what was over the rise.

Of course, there was still her mother's approval to get, but her father would help. She stepped from behind the little ABCO.

Before Fred could take her elbow, she hoisted herself into the automobile, grabbed Alberta's hand and pulled her to her feet. Raising their clasped hands, she announced, *"We are ready to race and* WE WILL WIN IN AN ABCO!"

Alberta just naturally joined her on, "EASY AS ABC!"

There were cheers and shouts of "You got Moxie,"

and "Give 'em a run, girls." There were also quite a few grins which nobody tried to hide.

The two fathers shook hands and slapped each other on the back. Then Mr. Philpot hurried toward the *Gazette* building and Mr. Cunningham took Fred outside to examine the big ABCO with an eye toward racing it. Everybody followed them, leaving Trudy and Alberta standing in the runabout.

"Well," said Alberta.

Trudy glared out the window at everyone crowding around her father's automobile, talking and nodding or listening to what Fred was telling Mr. Cunningham.

"Just wait until Papa writes the story for the *Gazette*," she said. "They'll remember us then."

"It won't matter," said Alberta. "We can still get out of it gracefully."

Trudy stared at her. "Why would we want to get out of it?"

"Trudy, ladies do not race automobiles."

"They don't try to vamp Fred Auklander, either."

Alberta giggled.

"Besides, we never had an automobile race before. How do we know they don't?" Trudy suspected her mother would know and tell her.

Quentin stuck his head in the door and said, "Hurry up, Trudy. You have to take this horse home."

Trudy folded her arms. "I'm a mechanician, not a groom."

Her brother made a rude noise.

Alberta said, "I think it's highly unsuitable for my

father's automobile racing team to be seen leading a horse around town."

She hardly stressed *my father*, but when she held out her hand, Quentin leaped to help her down from the ABCO. He just told Trudy, "Have you gone loony? This race is *serious*," and left her to get down by herself. She stepped on her skirts and tore the ruffle on her petticoat, which wasn't going to help her any with Mama.

They left by the back door, suspecting Quentin might repeat his order about the horse in front of all those people. They skirted Mr. Cunningham's Gentlemen's Speedy Sportster and reached the sidewalk where they could walk together.

Alberta said, "Want to stay overnight?"

"Just dinner, thank you." That would give Papa time to break the news to her mother, if somebody hadn't already, and argue away her objections before Trudy got home. Not that her mother would give up objecting, but the worst would be over. As always, Trudy added, "If Mrs. Webster doesn't mind."

They knew she wouldn't.

At Alberta's house, Alberta telephoned Trudy's, which was just across the street and three doors down. Trudy stepped into the kitchen and watched Mrs. Webster frost a plantation mint cake so Alberta could truthfully say she wasn't present in case Mama asked to speak to her. Bertha answered. Trudy knew because she heard Alberta leave a message. "Will you please tell Mrs. Philpot that Trudence is dining with the Cunninghams?"

Alberta came into the kitchen and nodded that it was

all right. They took pieces of cake up to Alberta's room and tried to guess what the ***s in the scandalous novel meant. They also wondered about the race, but they knew even less about automobiles than they did about "two natures vibrating as One" on a tiger-skin rug. So they heated Alberta's curling iron and did their hair *en pompadour* with ringlets at the sides and back. They decided they looked absolutely elegant and went down to dinner that way.

Mrs. Webster banged down the soup plates and rolled her eyes at the chandelier but Mr. Cunningham liked it. He held their chairs, called them Miss Philpot and Miss Cunningham and told them they were the greatest boost for steamers since the condensing boiler. Trudy remembered to sit straight, keep her elbows in and leave some food on her plate. Her mother would have been proud of her. Except for the pompadour.

Trudy took that down before she went home. When her mother wasn't telling her to remember her age, she was worrying about Trudy growing up too fast.

When Trudy opened the front door, her mother was saying, "Your sister and Fred Auklander? Whatever can you be thinking of?"

TWO

$\mathbf{M}$rs. Philpot must have heard Trudy's yelp or felt a draft because she called, "Is that you, Trudence?"

Trudy shut the door and stepped into the parlor. Only her mother and Quentin were there. Her father had gone to the San Julio Businessmen's Club with Mr. Cunningham. Trudy glared at her brother. If he was going to snitch, he should at least get it right. She wondered how she could deny any interest in Fred Auklander without incriminating Alberta.

She didn't have to. What her mother was objecting to, she soon learned, was a training program Quentin had worked out for the race. Alberta wasn't going to like it any better than Mrs. Philpot did. Quentin planned to teach Alberta to drive ABCOs while Fred taught Trudy how to repair them.

"When do I learn to drive?" said Trudy.

"You don't need to. You're the mechanician." Quentin gave her a hateful smirk.

Trudy flopped into a red velvet chair and glared.

"Sit up straight, Trudence," said Mrs. Philpot. Then,

21

to Quentin, "It's completely improper. Let Mr. Cunningham teach Alberta to drive and you can chaperone your sister."

Trudy didn't think that was any improvement. Neither would Alberta.

"Mr. Cunningham has to scout the route, arrange rooms for the girls." Quentin heaved a great sigh. "They've complicated everything. Let Papa or Mathias Jr. stay at the dealership with Trudy, they think this is so all-fired great for the *Gazette*."

Mrs. Philpot went on as if she hadn't heard. "I must also speak for Alberta since she has no mother of her own. And I cannot permit you to drive around the countryside with her unchaperoned."

"I'll go with them," said Trudy.

"There isn't time!" said Quentin.

"There is always time for propriety," said Mrs. Philpot.

Then she and Quentin began telling each other the same things in different ways until Mr. Philpot came home and settled the argument.

"Trudy and Alberta will chaperone each other," he said.

"There isn't time," repeated Quentin. "That automobile has to be completely checked, and if Trudy is going to learn anything at all, she has to be there. It's bad enough Fred can't work on it while she's in school, but if he has to wait for her while she chaperones Alberta's driving...."

Mr. Philpot waved him quiet. "I'll ask Madame

Butashky to release them from a few classes if it becomes necessary."

"I'm sure she'll oblige." Mrs. Philpot's voice was disapproving. "It's the sort of escapade that woman likes to encourage."

Trudy decided to retreat. She kissed her parents good-night, made a face at Quentin and went upstairs, marveling at how suddenly life could change. She'd gotten out of bed "Trudy Philpot: Her Father Owns the *Gazette*" and was climbing back in "Trudence Philpot: Automobile Racer."

She wondered about the race and if they'd win. If they did, would the mayor of Phoenix give them flower necklaces like the ones she'd seen in pictures of winning race horses? Or would they be carried on people's shoulders like Bill Ditweller when he struck out Gainesville at the Fourth of July picnic?

She was a long time getting to sleep and the last one down for breakfast.

As she entered the dining room, her mother was tapping her newspaper and saying, "This is what comes of sending her to that Academy."

Trudy kissed her mother's cheek and said, "Madame Butashky had nothing to do with it, Mama. It was the Fates. They wove the race into the thread of my life."

Quentin sounded as if he were gargling behind his copy of the *Gazette*.

As he leafed through his copy looking for errors, Mr. Philpot said, "There, you see, Harriet? They're teaching her Greek mythology at that Academy."

"And not a thing about domestic arts. Thread is spun, Trudence. Cloth is woven." As she spoke, Mrs. Philpot inspected Trudy from the ribbon holding back her hair to her high-buttoned boots. As usual, she frowned at the baggy serge bloomers.

After Rose Truex crashed and broke her arm, Madame Butashky had forbidden students to bicycle to the Academy unless they wore bloomers. When Mr. Philpot printed the ruling in the *Gazette,* letters to the editor set a new record. Madame had replied, pointing out quite correctly that long skirts were dangerous around sprockets and drive chains. There were more letters, the *Gazette*'s circulation jumped seventeen percent and four students were removed from the Academy. It would have been five if Mrs. Philpot had had her way.

Trudy moved around the table to her father, pausing at her own chair. Every morning since she'd finished McGuffey's Third Reader she'd found her own copy of the *Gazette* neatly folded beside her plate. This morning the newspaper was spread over her plate to show the spidery headlines above the racing story.

Trudy read them aloud. " 'Alberta Cunningham and Trudence Philpot, the World's First and Foremost Female Racing Team.' Does Alberta come first because she's the driver?"

"Because she's a Cunningham," said Mr. Philpot. "Your brother decided alphabetically was the only fair way."

He folded his newspaper and made notes on a pad beside his plate.

Trudy kissed him and said, "May I have your copy? I want to send a clipping to James." Her middle brother was a lawyer in Boston.

"Mathias Jr. left ten extra copies on the porch on his way home this morning. You and your mother may distribute those as you see fit."

Mrs. Philpot said, "I have no intention of publicizing this event."

"Harriet, the *purpose* of this event is publicity."

"The purpose of this event is winning," said Quentin. He folded his newspaper and leaned back so Bertha could serve his plate of ham and eggs. He scowled across the table at Trudy. "People buy automobiles that win races. The future of the ABCO dealership depends on this race."

"I know. Mr. Cunningham explained it last night." Trudy propped her *Gazette* on the sugar bowl so she could read it while she ate. She didn't repeat what Mr. Cunningham had said about other dealers selling more automobiles in one month than Quentin had in four. It wasn't her brother's fault. Since ex-Councilman Very had started selling Continentals ("Everything a Motor Car Should Be") from his barn, there were too many dealerships in San Julio. Added to that was the fact that people just didn't think steamers could stand up to gasoline engines. Winning the two-day race would prove they could. Even coming in second or third would help.

Looking straight at Quentin, Trudy added, "Mr. Cunningham says that with Alberta and me as his team, we just have to finish and sales will jump."

25

"*If* you finish. There are very good reasons, Trudy, why girls don't drive automobiles."

"Young ladies," Trudy corrected automatically, wishing Mama would let her put her hair up. "And Miss Dupree drives an automobile."

Besides talking to spirits on her psychophone, Miss Dupree wrote social news for the *Gazette*. Trudy often saw her boxy black automobile gliding down Main Street, fresh flowers in the bud vases that were fastened between the plate-glass windows.

"An electric." Quentin waved it aside with a piece of toast. Electrics couldn't go fast enough or far enough on batteries to be considered real automobiles.

"Mr. Cunningham says an ABCO is just as easy to drive."

Mr. Philpot said, "So did Quentin when he was trying to sell me one."

"Mathias," Mrs. Philpot warned.

But for once Quentin didn't pick up the argument. He told Trudy, "Suppose you have a flat tire?"

"I fix my bicycle tires all the time."

She'd even seen Alberta fix one when they were two miles out of town with no male to offer to do it for her. She was slower than Trudy but made a neater patch.

"Automobile tires are different," said Quentin.

"They don't look different, just bigger."

"Wait until you have to change one."

"Mathias," said Mrs. Philpot, "I cannot permit this. They'll be stranded in the desert and die of thirst or snakebite."

"Now, Harriet, we went over all this at dinner last night." Slowly and patiently, like Miss Peterson explaining genus and species for the fifth time, Mr. Philpot said, "Every checkpoint and refueling stop will have a worry wagon. If an entry is overdue, the wagon will go out looking for it. Also, the last California checkpoint, the last one before Yuma, is on the railroad. From there on into Phoenix, every town will be on the railroad and the telegraph. They *cannot* be stranded." He held his hand up, palm out.

"And let's not hear any more about the overnight stop in Yuma. Bert's going to find them a hotel. They will not be lodged with the other teams. Bert and I have worked...."

The doorbell clattered. Holding onto the table edge, Trudy tipped her chair back on two legs so she could watch Bertha open the door. Mrs. Philpot wasn't so intent on her husband's reexplanation of sleeping accommodations that she didn't notice. She gave Trudy a warning look. Trudy let her chair down with a thump and went back to fried eggs and the newspaper story.

Alberta came in carrying her own copy of the *Gazette* and wearing a blue wool cheviot skirt and a white shirtwaist with fifty million tucks in the front. Trudy groaned.

Mrs. Philpot smiled and said, "You look lovely this morning, Alberta."

"Thank you." She good-morninged everyone and told Mr. Philpot how wonderful the story was. "I'm going to buy a leather-covered scrapbook and save it forever!" She slid into the chair next to Quentin and told Trudy, "I came early so you'd have time to change."

"I don't want to change."

"But everybody will be watching us today. We must look our best." Alberta's opinion of bloomers was almost as low as Mrs. Philpot's.

Trudy pushed her plate aside. "We'll have to walk and these boots aren't broken in yet."

Mr. Philpot said, "If you hurry, I'll drive you in the carriage."

"We'll still have to walk home."

"Oh, no," said Quentin. "No detours. You come straight to the dealership from now on."

"*The dealership?*" Alberta looked as if she'd been given a three-day shopping trip to Los Angeles, complete with train ticket.

"You have to learn to drive," Quentin told her.

"I better change," Trudy said and skedaddled before Alberta learned it wasn't Fred Auklander who'd be doing the teaching. She almost ran down Bertha, who was bringing a plate of toast and a coffee cup for Alberta.

"Automobiling!" Bertha muttered. "I thought she'd have more sense even if you don't."

"We're in the twentieth century now, Bertha. And I'll have another cup of coffee with my driver."

Mrs. Philpot only allowed Trudy one cup a day, at breakfast, and worried about that spoiling her complexion, which was silly. Alberta drank coffee all the time and her complexion was perfect.

When Trudy came back in skirt and shirtwaist, her

cup had been refilled. She smiled and decided to ask again about putting up her hair. But her mother and Bertha had ways of winning while losing. The coffee was boiling hot with no room to add milk. And before it could cool enough to be sipped, Bertha came in to say, "Henry's bringing the carriage around, Mr. Philpot," and went to get his derby.

Trudy and Alberta scrambled for jackets, books and pencil boxes. Mrs. Philpot followed them into the hall and made them promise never to be separated while engaged in racing activities.

"For your own protection," she warned.

Alberta looked alarmed but there wasn't time to explain, not with Mr. Philpot waiting to hand them into the carriage. Mrs. Philpot went onto the porch with them, saying for the third time how nice they looked in skirts.

A dining room window was raised and Quentin yelled, "I think it's highly unsuitable for an automobile racing team to be riding in a carriage."

"I agree," Trudy called back. It had already occurred to her that somebody, probably Suzanne Davenport, would say something similar. "But the owner of this carriage has sacrificed his automobile to the greater glory of ABCOs."

Quentin's two-word answer sent their mother back into the house. The dining room window banged shut as the horses clopped forward. Trudy laughed and waved, though she doubted that Quentin had time to be watching.

Alberta was right about people noticing them. The milkman ladling milk into Mrs. Rhinebeck's pitcher, the ice man, the policeman, Mr. Potter setting his crates of vegetables onto the sidewalk, everyone who'd read the *Gazette* and knew them by sight waved and wished them luck. A few asked if the story was true, which made Mr. Philpot bristle.

It was much the same at the Academy, except for Suzanne Davenport who told everyone it was just an advertising trick and they'd back out before the race started. Trudy was surprised at how many believed her, including a few teachers. She guessed the same thought was behind some of the stares and knowing smiles they received on Main Street after school.

George Doty, bicycling down the opposite side of the street, called, "Hey, kiddos, you expecting to win that race?"

Alberta pretended not to see him, but Trudy turned to call back, "Easy as ABC!"

George narrowly missed Mrs. Hubble's buggy as he yelled over his shoulder, "That's what you think!" George was the mechanician for the Ford ("Don't foot it —Ford it!") dealership.

"Was that a threat?" muttered Alberta.

Trudy laughed. "Are you going to give him another black eye if it was?"

Alberta pretended not to hear. "Look! The Bon Ton has a new spring suit in the window. Look at the skirt!"

It came only to the anklebone.

"Sensible," said Trudy.

"Daring," said Alberta. "Let's try one on."

"Better not. Quentin told us to hurry."

They stopped at the Ice Cream Emporium to fortify themselves with cherry Cokes. Mr. Rhodamoyer asked a lot of questions about ABCOs. Trudy couldn't tell if he was testing her or teasing her, but she could answer them all from what she'd heard at the breakfast table. It worried her that she'd picked up so much without wanting to, even if it was useful. Then Mrs. Hubble and her sister from Gainesville came in for ice cream sodas and asked if they weren't worried or frightened.

"Of course not," Trudy told them. "It's no different from driving to Gainesville in a carriage, just longer and safer because there aren't any horses to bolt."

The next stop was the drugstore. They had to browse for fifteen minutes before Miss Timson left the toiletries counter and Alberta could sneak sample dabs of "Nuit d'Amour."

Then Miss Dupree stopped her electric at the curb to give them a psychophone message from Queen Elizabeth: "All yieldeth to perseverance." Which was about what Madame Butashky had told them in more modern English. When they finally reached the ABCO dealership, Quentin was furious.

He met them at the door and tried to shout in a whisper. "Where have you been? I've been waiting and waiting! Your father's here today. I can start your driving lessons."

They could see Mr. Cunningham in his glass-paneled office shouting into the telephone. He put down the earpiece and clasped his hands over his head like a prize fighter. Trudy and Alberta smiled and waved back. Alberta blew a kiss.

Mr. Philpot's big ABCO had been brought inside. The touring model looked huge and cumbersome among the sportsters and runabouts. Fred had removed the hood and rear deck and was explaining steam engines to three men and a half-dozen boys. Having listened to Fred the day before, Trudy wasn't surprised when his audience showed more interest in her and Alberta. But the way the men stared was disconcerting. She didn't blame Alberta for hanging back when Quentin tried to lead them in that direction.

She said, "We'll go home and wait until you put it together."

"What?" said Quentin. "Oh, that. Nobody drives the entry until the race. We've ordered another tourer so you can get the feel of it, but until it arrives you'll have to drive a sportster. Hurry up!"

He shooed them into the alley, but when he got up on the seat beside Alberta, there wasn't room for all of Trudy. Fred's audience had deserted him and followed the team into the alley. They grinned at Trudy's efforts to make herself fit.

"It's all these petticoats," she said. "If we'd worn our bl——"

"Bicycling costumes," interrupted Alberta. "Let's go change."

They climbed down and were halfway out the alley before Quentin recovered enough to yell, "Thirty minutes in front of Alberta's house. *And you better be ready!*"

The men were laughing. One of them said in a falsetto, "Oh, Mr. Starter, hold the gun. I simply can't race without my pink parasol."

Trudy stomped away, her face hot. Alberta kept repeating all the reasons they had to race, more for herself than for Trudy.

They were ready on time, but the baggy knee-length bloomers didn't make enough difference.

"You'll have to wait here," Quentin told Trudy.

"I have to go."

"You don't."

"I DO!"

"She does," said Alberta. "We made a solemn and sacred promise to your mother. If Trudy doesn't go, then neither can I."

Quentin turned to look at the sun and through clenched teeth said, "There isn't room!"

"I'll sit on the rear deck," said Trudy.

"You'll fall off and break your head. What will Mama say then about your sacred promise?"

"What about that smooth ride you brag about?"

"The *steam engine* has no vibration, but *roads* have bumps and ruts!"

"It's getting late," Trudy reminded him.

That started an argument about who had wasted the most time. They made enough noise to attract the five Martin kids and cause Mrs. Schmidt's parlor curtain to move aside. Trudy glanced nervously at her own porch and cut Quentin off by climbing onto the deck. The metal was warm from the burners but not uncomfortable. She knelt behind the seat, gripping its back, and peered between her brother and Alberta.

"All right," said Quentin. "Just get the feel of driving an automobile. It's all we have time for, anyhow. That's the throttle. The more you open it, the faster you'll go. The pedal on the right is to stop, the one on the left for reverse. That's backing up."

"She knows what reverse means," Trudy told him. "Good God."

The Martin kids laughed, all except the youngest who had both index fingers in his mouth.

Quentin fiddled with some valves, then said, "Open the throttle. Slowly."

Trudy tightened her grip. Alberta reached for the little brass gadget beside the steering column, and the automobile glided silently away from the curb. The Martin kids cheered and waved, all except the youngest. Trudy grinned and waved back.

Up and down the streets they went. The ride was so smooth and slow that Trudy turned around and sat cross-legged with her back to the seat. People they passed were startled to see her sitting there like a sultan. They laughed and waved or called warnings. Some of the bicyclists followed, asking questions about the race. It was better than the morning's carriage ride.

As they neared Main Street there were more people, many on bicycles and most headed home. Trudy was so busy playing The World's First Female Racing Mechanician that she didn't see what hit them.

THREE

Trudy fell over and went skidding across the deck, frantically grabbing for a handhold. She didn't find one but as she slid over the side her bloomers caught on a brass handle. They tore slowly, lowering her gently to the ground on her hands and knees. She scrambled to her feet and, holding the rip together with one hand, went around the ABCO to see what the shouting was about.

A young typist bicycling home from work and admiring the spring suit in the Bon Ton's window had run into the ABCO on Quentin's side. Nobody was hurt but the front wheel of the bicycle was a mess. Quentin was making rude remarks about the young lady's eyesight while she told him that automobiles should be heard as well as seen.

"Even horses give fair warning," she was shouting.

Some people in the gathering crowd agreed. Others didn't, but all tried to share their opinions with the policeman who came to sort out the blame. Somebody in one of the stores must have done a lot of telephoning. Mr. Philpot and Mathias Jr. arrived right behind the policeman, and Mr. Cunningham soon drove up in his ABCO, his lawyer beside him. Dr. Gosser followed in his buggy.

Alberta, who'd been sitting stiff and white-faced, started crying when her father lifted her down. Doc Gosser gave Mr. Cunningham a sleeping powder for her, saw them off in Mr. Cunningham's sportster and then added his opinion to the crowd's.

Quentin moved over behind the steering wheel. Trudy climbed up and took the passenger seat. It saved having to hold her bloomers together and gave her a good view.

Mr. Cunningham's lawyer soothed the young typist with ten dollars for a new bicycle and then had everybody sign a paper. Mathias Jr. rushed around taking statements, trying to get a story in the next editiion.

The next day was Saturday, but Bertha shook Trudy awake earlier than on school days.

"Telephone," she said. "Your daredevil driver wants to talk to you."

Trudy pulled on her kimono and went downstairs.

"Did you read it?" Alberta's voice was full of despair.

"Read what?"

"About the accident!"

"Wait a minute." Trudy let the earpiece dangle from its cord and went into the dining room for her copy of the *Gazette*. Bertha was setting out dishes of jam, butter and marmalade.

"He buried it on the next-to-last page," she told Trudy, "where it rightfully belongs."

Bertha read her copy of the *Gazette* carefully and with almost as critical an eye as Mr. Philpot. She pushed

36

through the kitchen door saying, "Bloomers and automobiles," in exactly the same tone Madame Butashky used for corsets and restaurants that refused to seat unescorted females.

Trudy found the article and read it on the way back to the telephone. She didn't see anything to be upset about even when Alberta read the offending words.

"A twenty-year-old *spinster*," Alberta wailed.

"That's just to let readers know she isn't married."

"He already did that." Alberta read again, "*Miss* Hacker, a twenty-year-old spinster. . . . I called him, Trudy."

A draft under the front door kept the floorboards cold. Trudy tried to warm one bare foot on top of the other. "Called who?"

"Mathias Jr.! I asked, 'At what age does a young lady become a spinster?' And he said, 'Approximately nineteen years, eleven months, twenty-nine days and eleven hours, give or take a few minutes.' "

Trudy laughed.

"It is not funny, Trudy. And it isn't fair!"

Trudy hadn't thought about it before but Alberta was right. It was long skirts at sixteen, then up with the hair and down the aisle, like Francine Decker who hadn't finished her second year at the Academy.

"It certainly doesn't give us much time, does it?" she said.

"No. It takes months to organize a proper wedding."

"I wasn't thinking about getting married. I meant other things."

"What things?"

"I don't know." What had the beautiful countess been doing until the handsome young man arrived? But she couldn't talk about that with her mother coming down the stairs.

Mrs. Philpot stopped to kiss Trudy's cheek and ask how she felt. Then she said, "If that's Alberta, invite her to breakfast."

"I heard," said Alberta. "I'll be right over."

"Good," said Trudy. "You can help me decide what female mechanicians wear."

Everything Trudy owned seemed too shabby or too new. They decided on a skirt she was outgrowing. It wasn't quite as short as the one in the Bon Ton's window, a point Trudy could use if her mother objected. The shirtwaist was much newer but had an ink stain on the left sleeve.

"It won't show when I roll up the sleeves," she told the fussing Alberta.

"In *public*?"

"A ball's public and we'll show a lot more than bare arms wearing ball gowns."

"That's different."

"I don't see how. Come on, we're missing breakfast."

Quentin was reading a letter to the *Gazette*. They could hear him from the top of the stairs. The letter warned of the dangers of silent vehicles sneaking up on innocent citizens and demanded that the council pass an ordinance requiring noiseless automobiles to ring bells while moving inside San Julio city limits.

"But the bicycle ran into us." Trudy kissed her father and slid onto her chair. "They should put the bells on bicycles."

Quentin stabbed his finger at the newspaper. "I hardly think this letter was written out of concern for safety. It's signed by ex-Councilman Very's brother-in-law, though I doubt if he wrote it."

Mr. Philpot sighed. "Ex-Councilman Very is a vindictive man. Could I have some more toast, Bertha?"

"Fast, too," said Quentin, "to get the letter written and delivered in time for this morning's edition. I just wonder why it was printed."

"Thank you, Bertha. Every *Gazette* reader has a right to express an opinion."

"You don't have to print it!"

"It is the policy of the *Gazette* to be fair and objective."

"*Fair?*"

Mrs. Philpot said, "But those automobiles are dangerous, Quentin. Look at Trudy and Alberta."

Trudy stopped her fork in midair, staring over it at Alberta. Alberta calmly buttered a slice of toast.

Quentin threw his napkin on top of the newspaper. "I hope you don't go saying that at your club meetings, Mama. Between you and Papa, I won't have a job."

"Oh, dear." Mrs. Philpot looked as distressed as she'd sounded the night before.

Trudy concentrated on her breakfast. From the way Quentin and her father were raising their voices, she wasn't going to have much time to eat.

"I'll remind you," said Mr. Philpot, "that I was here last night, giving aid and assistance." To you, his look at Quentin said.

"And receiving telephone calls! Mathias Jr. wouldn't have printed that letter without your approval!" Quentin pushed back his chair and stood up.

"Come on, you two," he ordered and stalked out.

Trudy shoved half a fried egg in her mouth as she rose.

"*Trudence!*" said her mother.

Alberta slapped jam on the slice of toast and gave it to Trudy as they ran after Quentin.

They reached the ABCO dealership half an hour early. Quentin used the time teaching Alberta how to get up steam and reverse. Trudy sat on an empty packing case and watched the sportster scoot up and down the alley, as fast in reverse as forward. At seven o'clock Fred Auklander arrived and Trudy began her training.

That Saturday and the next and the after-school sessions in between were so much alike that Trudy and Alberta couldn't always agree on what happened which day.

Fred was as dull as Trudy had expected. He explained everything, even fusable plugs which the new boilers didn't need. Trudy kept telling him she didn't need to know why things worked, just how to fix them when they didn't. But Fred explained anyhow and Alberta listened wide-eyed when there weren't any visitors around, which wasn't very often.

Every man and boy with an interest in the race and

time to spare came to inspect the entry and its team. They asked questions and offered advice, none of it useful and little of it funny. Quentin kept things in proper bounds, but there were still some leers and winks or sniggers at remarks Alberta and Trudy couldn't hear. It made them uncomfortable.

Alberta retreated to the running board nearest Trudy and read magazines borrowed from Mrs. Webster, but Trudy refused to be cowed. She played Madame Butashky or her mother at her most proper, depending on who was standing around the ABCO. She rather enjoyed it but that, too, became part of the sameness of the training.

A few events broke the routine. Mrs. Philpot visited the dealership to check the proprieties, escorted by Mathias Jr. and his oldest boy. Trudy's nephew asked more questions than Mr. Rhodamoyer at the Ice Cream Emporium. Mrs. Philpot seemed interested, too. At least she made no more objections to Quentin's training program. That might have been because Mathias Jr. had warned them of the visit and Quentin had eased most of the gawking men outside. Or it could have been the signs that appeared at the other four dealerships: "Be safe, not sorry! Give fair warning! Drive an automobile with a gasoline engine!" They threatened Quentin's security as much as the race threatened Trudy's. Not that any of the dealers were selling automobiles. Everybody in San Julio and Gainesville was waiting for the results of the race.

Madame Butashky swooped into the dealership unannounced, first with Miss Peterson and again alone. Both

times the gawkers looked as uncomfortable as they sometimes made Alberta and Trudy feel. And one evening
Miss Dupree was waiting outside in her electric with a
message from Catherine the Great: "March on! The
snow shall fade!"

Trudy thought advice from Casey Jones or some
Roman chariot racer might have been more helpful but
Alberta was delighted. She insisted the message meant
racing would ruin Trudy's hands and told Miss Timson
at the drugstore about it. That gave them an excuse to
stop in each day. Trudy would maneuver Miss Timson
out of the way so Alberta could sample the "Nuit
d'Amour." She'd tried to buy a bottle but Miss Timson
had refused to sell it.

"Completely unsuitable for a girl of your age," she'd
told Alberta. "You should use the Florida Water."

For all the effect "Nuit d'Amour" had on Fred
Auklander, she might as well have.

"That's because a tiny dab doesn't waft me on clouds
of scent," said Alberta, quoting from the scandalous
novel. "I need a bottle."

Quentin was so short-tempered they didn't dare ask
him to buy one. As a return favor, he'd probably ask
them to quit the race.

He gave Alberta driving lessons each evening from
closing until dusk. Trudy learned by watching from the
rear deck, though it wasn't quite as easy as ABC. The
driver had half a dozen gauges to watch, with screw valves
to control the flow of gasoline to the burner that heated
the water, the crucial mixture of water and steam in the

boiler and the temperature and pressure. There was a correct starting order that anybody (except Mr. Philpot, apparently) could memorize, but to get the best from an ABCO, the variables had to be adjusted as the road and driving conditions changed. A good driver had a feel for the mix required, and Alberta surprised Quentin by having it.

"Just like a man," he kept saying.

Trudy didn't tell him that Alberta thought of it as mixing her famous punch, which had to be adjusted according to the age of the guests and the fruit available. Quentin was cranky enough as it was.

Alberta needed a touring model to practice with, and the one ordered didn't arrive. The weekend before the race, Quentin telephoned the station after every westbound train. He could have saved bothering the operator and stationmaster. Mr. Philpot was meeting most trains to welcome newspapermen, not just those he'd expected from Yuma and Phoenix or hoped for from Los Angeles and San Francisco. Eastern newspapers, too, were sending representatives to report on the female racing team.

Monday morning, Trudy dressed to go to the ABCO dealership. Madame Butashky had excused her and Alberta from classes so they could concentrate on preparing for Friday. Trudy wore her old skirt and stained shirtwaist to breakfast, but Alberta telephoned, as planned.

Trudy asked her mother, "May I be excused, please? Alberta needs me."

Her mother gave permission.

Quentin said, "Try to get to the dealership before noon."

Trudy didn't wait to make a face. She grabbed her jacket and headed for Alberta's and the unstained shirtwaist with picot trim she'd left there the day before. Alberta loaned her some Florida Water. They powdered their noses with cornstarch and headed for the dealership and the newspapermen.

"From Chicago, Detroit and St. Louis," chanted Trudy. "Maybe even *New York!*"

She had pictured men like James or Mathias Jr. but with the polished look of the man in the Arrow Shirt advertisements. They were as old as her father and looked more like the men who lounged in front of the pool hall or on the Civil War statue in the square. Their clothes had a newer cut but were rumpled and uncared for. They talked faster and used strange words but their questions and jokes were the same ones Trudy had been hearing for a week. She didn't know how she could stand three more full days. And Alberta was reduced to reading *The Automobile Maker and Dealer,* which she'd found in her father's office.

Fred rescued them. Tuesday morning he wiped his hands on a greasy rag and announced the ABCO was race-ready except for the special wheels Mr. Cunningham was bringing from Los Angeles.

The newspapermen rushed to the other dealerships to see how nearly finished the other mechanicians were. Though they'd been working full days, they were still checking bits and pieces of their gasoline engines. And would be, Fred said, right up until Thursday evening.

Trudy expected Alberta to find excuses to linger at the dealership now that Fred was free to read magazines, too. But she was as eager as Trudy to be away. They had shopping to do and final fittings with Mrs. Philpot's dressmaker. There was to be a Race Gala at a hotel in Phoenix Saturday night. Win or lose, Trudy and Alberta were going to wear their first formal gowns. And Mrs. Philpot had agreed it was time to put up their hair. The only question was when.

They'd decided it was practical to wait until after the race. But that was before their visit to the Bon Ton. Alberta tried on a new large hat with a motoring veil that tied under the chin. It didn't sit right without a pompadour and she changed her mind about waiting for the Gala.

They argued about it in Mrs. Philpot's sewing room while they stitched ruffles inside their shirtwaists to give their bosoms a fashionable pouter-pigeon shape. At least, Alberta sewed. Trudy's roughened hands kept catching in the silk. She sat on the floor clipping race stories from two identical stacks of out-of-town newspapers. Alberta pasted hers in a leather-covered scrapbook but Trudy filed hers in folders from her father's office, ready for when she wrote her memoirs: *Trudy Philpot, Daredevil Racer.* Unless she took up ballooning or something. Then she'd call it *Trudence Philpot, Female Extraordinaire.*

The telephone interrupted their pompadour debate. Alberta stopped stitching to count the rings. Bertha and Mrs. Webster had the afternoon off and Mrs. Philpot was at the League for Civic Improvement.

"Yours," said Alberta.

Trudy got to her feet and stepped carefully over the clippings. "Probably Quentin, ordering us back to ABCO and duty."

It was. The tourer had finally arrived and he wanted to continue the driving lessons.

"Now?" said Trudy.

"No, not now. Can't leave the dealership without a salesman." He was shouting so loud that Alberta, leaning over the banister, could hear when Trudy held out the earpiece. "But you two better get down here right away. Some photographers came on the same train and I don't want any picture-taking interfering with the driving lesson. It's IMPORTANT and we don't have much time left!"

He hung up without saying good-by. Trudy put the receiver on the hook and looked up at Alberta. Alberta looked back.

Trudy sighed. "All right. I'm sure Mama won't mind if we borrow her curling iron."

They also borrowed all her spare combs and hairpins and one of her parasols. Trudy had only one hat, a straw sailor she wore only when she had to. She was glad to let Alberta wear it. Though parasols were going out of fashion, she felt quite grand and elegant strolling down Main Street with her mother's over her shoulder.

Gentlemen they didn't know smiled and tipped their hats. Women stared and whispered and would probably try to telephone Mrs. Philpot. Suzanne Davenport and Margaret Bowers pretended not to recognize them, but Mr. Rhodamoyer insisted on serving their Cokes at a table. Unfortunately, Quentin had seen them and came to drag them away before they were finished.

He'd parked the new ABCO in the street so the dealership name would show in the photographs. Quite a crowd gathered to watch Trudy and Alberta pose in the ABCO, beside it, with one foot on the running board, getting in and getting out, together and singly. The photographers wanted Quentin to remove the hood so Trudy could pretend to repair the boiler.

"Automobile boilers do not explode," said Quentin. He took out his pocket watch and said, "Time to close. Sorry, gentlemen."

He locked the dealership door and climbed into the front seat. He directed Alberta to the outskirts of town Trudy sat in the center of the rear seat, parasol over her shoulder, and pretended she was Lillian Russell. She wouldn't mind having her photograph taken every day.

When Alberta had the feel of the larger automobile, Quentin had her drive out of town for what he called diversified motoring experience. That meant driving up and down steep banks, fording creeks flooded with spring runoff and skidding around a patch of gravel behind the gas plant. Trudy bounced on the rear seat, trying to keep from falling out and whooping like a cowboy. It was her idea of racing. But Alberta hunched over the wheel, her face grim and her knuckles white.

They lost the boys who always followed them on bicycles, but their place was taken by newspapermen in a Model Automobile ("Hills and Sand Become Level Land") rented from the Gregory stables. The Gregorys,

Jr. and Sr., sold as well as leased Models and were entered in the race. Trudy was delighted when the Model couldn't keep up on Harmon's hill.

She gripped the furled parasol between her knees and turned to yell through cupped hands, "Get an ABCO! Easy as ABC!"

"Don't gloat," Quentin told her. "That automobile's carrying a lot of weight. The Gregorys are racing a sportster and it's mostly downhill to Phoenix."

"Bushwa," said Trudy, and braced for the downhill run.

All the skidding and jouncing had loosened the pins and combs in the pompadours. Trudy felt hanks of hair fall loose, like worms or snakes sliding down from her head. The straw hat was tilted over Alberta's left ear. She tugged it off and handed it back to Trudy.

"We look awful," she wailed.

Only she didn't. She reminded Trudy of the picture of Circe in their Greek mythology book. But she refused to let Quentin drive the ABCO back to the agency.

"I'm driving us home first," she told him. "If anybody sees us, I want them to know the reason we look this way."

Trudy tried to repin her own hair but most of the pins and combs were lost. She held the parasol more carefully and hoped her mother wouldn't mind.

Alberta chose back streets, taking such a roundabout way that the gaslights were lit before they finally stopped in front of the Cunningham house. Alberta started to say something to Quentin, then stared past him.

Trudy turned to see a man step from the porch. He looked exactly the way Trudy had expected an eastern newspaperman to look. As he neared, she saw he was young, about Quentin's age. And when he smiled up at her, it was the nicest smile Trudy had ever seen.

"Miss Cunningham?" he said.

Trudy shook her head and pointed the parasol at Alberta's back. Then she jumped from the opposite side of the ABCO and ran for home. She slammed her bedroom door behind her and leaned on the bureau to catch her breath. When she raised her head and looked in the mirror, it was even worse than she'd feared. Alberta might look like a windblown Circe but Trudy's hair looked like Medusa's.

"Damn," she said and threw herself on the bed.

FOUR

His name was John Baxter and he was in James's old room unpacking. Trudy learned that much from Bertha when she came to call Trudy to the telephone.

"Tell Alberta I'm not leaving my room until Friday morning," said Trudy.

"You're going to get mighty hungry," Bertha told her. "I'm not toting trays when you aren't sick."

But she must have delivered some kind of message because ten minutes later Alberta was tapping on Trudy's door and telling her, "I was so mortified, meeting Mr. Baxter that way! I don't know how I'll face him again."

"We could eat dinner at your house," Trudy suggested.

"Mrs. Webster isn't prepared. I've been invited here."

Alberta preened in front of the mirror, patting the waves in her hair. It was down again, brushed back and held with a wide black ribbon, but she was wearing one of the fluffy-ruffle shirtwaists and about a gallon of Florida Water. She didn't know much more about John Baxter than Bertha did.

"He's somebody Daddy met back east," she told Trudy. "He came for the race but of course he can't stay with us, not when Daddy's in Los Angeles. So Quentin very kindly offered hospitality. Hurry up, Trudy! We'll be late for dinner."

Trudy sighed and got off the bed. She banged drawers and kicked boots and pulled savagely on her comb until Alberta took it from her and arranged her hair, making wispy curls over the ears so it looked almost like a pompadour. She felt much better until Quentin saw them coming downstairs and laughed at her ruffle-filled shirtwaist.

She was delighted to find John Baxter next to her at the table until she realized it meant he'd be looking at Alberta all during dinner. Trudy decided to remain regally aloof, but she couldn't resist asking, "Do you live in New York City, Mr. Baxter?"

He turned and smiled that wonderful smile. "No. Boston."

"And no, he doesn't know James," Quentin put in.

"You with the *Herald*?" said Mr. Philpot, leaning back so Bertha could serve the soup.

"Loosely affiliated."

"Oh."

Trudy had to smile at her father's expression. He thought free-lance journalists lacked conviction and loyalty, but up until now, newspapers in Chicago and Detroit had been the most eastern ones represented.

"I understand you helped to organize the race," prompted John Baxter.

And the race and the qualities of the five entries were all that was talked about during dinner. Trudy ate little, keeping her hands in her lap as much as possible. They'd worried Alberta and her mother more than they had her. Scrubbing with a brush and laundry soap had gotten most of the grease off and what was left showed people like Suzanne Davenport that she was serious about the race. But she couldn't help being ashamed at how terrible they looked against the white linen tablecloth.

After dinner they rolled back the parlor rug and Quentin, Trudy and Alberta took turns pumping "The Maple Leaf Rag" through the player piano while John Baxter taught them the new ragtime dances. In spite of her mechanician hands, John danced once more with Trudy than he did with Alberta. But Trudy didn't get a chance to ask if he'd ever danced in New York or gone to the Trocadero or the Palladium.

Mr. Cunningham arrived the next day with the special wheels. He'd ridden all the way from Los Angeles in the baggage car with them. There were six, complete with tires. Two were to be carried in the rear seat of the ABCO with other emergency gear Fred and Quentin had been collecting. Trudy helped Fred put the other four on the ABCO.

Quentin had been right about automobile tires. Even with the special detachable rims and Alberta's help, changing one wasn't going to be easy or fast. She began to worry that Quentin might be right about other things, too.

The photographers took pictures of her changing the

wheels (Fred went over every nut and bolt), but that didn't make up for missing Alberta's driving lesson, especially since John Baxter went with Alberta and her father.

After being photographed in all kinds of poses that nobody who'd ever changed an automobile wheel would believe, Trudy got permission from Quentin to use Mr. Cunningham's office. She telephoned Rosemary Rasmussen, heard all the news from the Academy and learned that this week Rosemary was holding a ping-pong championship. Trudy accepted an invitation to that evening's match for herself and Alberta.

The race committee was holding a dinner for the newspapermen and photographers, the dealers and the race teams—all except Trudy and Alberta. Women were not allowed in the Businessmen's Club. Trudy didn't intend to sit home while Quentin and John Baxter went to a race party.

Alberta didn't play ping-pong but she was delighted with the invitation. It gave them a chance to show off the ragtime dance steps and politely brag about their training. Trudy exaggerated Alberta's steeplechase driving and Alberta managed to make Trudy's mechanicianing sound mysterious and dangerous. They both pretended the photographers were a trial and a nuisance. Trudy almost wished Suzanne Davenport had been invited.

She made cocoa when she got home, ran up and down stairs to consult with her mother about what to pack for Phoenix and telephoned Alberta twice, but she couldn't dawdle long enough to see John Baxter and Quentin come home. When she got down to breakfast they were already gone. So was her father.

Her mother repeated a long list of dos and don'ts, mostly don'ts, on their overnight stay in Yuma. The passengers on the Howdy Special, the train Stubby O'Dell had organized, seemed to worry her the most. She didn't hold a very high opinion of Stubby O'Dell, and the passengers were greeting the racers in Yuma with a barbecue. Mrs. Philpot seemed concerned about their conduct around young ladies.

"Under the circumstances," she kept saying.

Trudy nodded at appropriate times while she ate, then excused herself to let Alberta in, saying Bertha was busy preparing for Phoenix. She returned by way of the kitchen, hoping to get the coffee server, but Bertha handed her a cup already filled for Alberta.

"I'm putting my hair up in Phoenix," Trudy told her.

"You threatening or complaining?" said Bertha.

The only answer Trudy could think of was one overheard around the ABCO and that would only get her in trouble with Mama. She swept through the swing door with the dignity of a much-photographed mechanician and slopped most of Alberta's coffee into the saucer. Trudy poured it back in the cup and set it down in front of Alberta.

"There, it's all saucered and blowed," she told her.

"Trudence," said her mother, but mildly. She was busy checking a list and worrying about the girls' gowns being delivered in time to get the trunks to the station.

54

Trudy and Alberta were taking only what they needed overnight in Yuma. Everything else was going on the train with Mrs. Philpot and Bertha. As it turned out, Trudy and Alberta had plenty of time to collect their gowns from the dressmaker.

The afternoon's Grand Procession down Main Street to the San Julio Opera and Civic Hall, where the five automobiles were to be inspected and locked under guard until morning, was postponed. The newspapermen and gawkers shuttled between ex-Councilman Very's barn and the Stoddard-Dayton ("Six Cylinders—all in Action") dealership. Neither entry was race-ready until almost dark.

The entries were to meet at the train station. John Baxter helped Fred open the barn doors and Quentin drove the large ABCO into the alley. Then Alberta took his place behind the wheel and Trudy climbed up beside her. It was the first time Alberta had driven without Quentin or her father. She looked the way she had before her first jump into the Gregorys' haymow from one of the stable's crossbeams.

Quentin locked the dealership doors and waved them forward.

It was dark in the alley. Quentin on one side and Fred on the other guided the ABCO to the street. It was lighter there, but Quentin and Fred walked beside the automobile to the station where Mr. Cunningham was arguing about the ABCO's place in the procession.

The committee had decided on alphabetical order, but ex-Councilman Very wanted the owner's name used instead of the automobile's. Trudy couldn't hear what arguments he used, but he won. It put his Continental last but Will Becker's Ford led instead of the ABCO.

"Papa said he was a spiteful man," murmured Trudy.

"It doesn't matter," whispered Alberta. "I'm glad I don't have to lead."

It was dark when Stubby O'Dell finally waved the procession forward, spacing them carefully. First the bicycle policemen to clear the road, then the B.O.R.P. band, blaring offbeat when Trudy could hear them over the noise of the gasoline engines. The Ford was next, George Doty grinning on the seat beside Mr. Becker.

"Don't get used to first place," Trudy yelled at him. "It's the last time you'll be there."

"Trudy!" said Alberta, sounding much like Mrs. Philpot. Then she adjusted the throttle, released the brake pedal and they glided after the little red Ford.

All the automobiles had lights of some kind but they weren't to be wasted. Or depended on, either, Fred had warned Trudy. A pair of torchbearers flanked each entry and three pairs marched beside the band. Fred's torch wavered and dropped as he bent to listen or inspect something on the ABCO. Quentin marched on the other side, near Alberta. Bicyclists rode alongside or behind. As they turned onto Main Street, a cold wind bent the torch flames. Trudy turned up her jacket collar and did the same for Alberta, who refused to take a hand from the wheel or her eyes from the Ford's silhouette.

The crowd along Main Street surprised Trudy, and most of the people she saw under the gas lamps were strangers. She hadn't realized how many the race had brought to San Julio. Most of them paid admission to the Opera and Civic Hall to watch the inspection, pushing against the red velvet ropes that kept a clear space around each automobile.

"We should have had one of these ropes at the dealership," said Alberta.

She and Mrs. Philpot, who had joined them, treated the velvet circle as a receiving line, greeting and talking with people they knew or recognized. Trudy was left with the strangers, answering questions about the ABCO, mostly from women who were curious but didn't know the right questions to ask.

After an hour of trial and success, she found herself telling half a dozen women, "You've lit coal oil stoves, haven't you? This burner is much the same. And this burner is even easier to light because it has a pilot light. And you've all mixed cakes or biscuits, haven't you? Mixing the fuel isn't much different." She gave a brief list of starting procedures and ended, "You come out tomorrow and watch these gentlemen trying to start their smelly gasoline engines, cranking and sweating"—after a hard look from her mother she changed the word to "perspiring"—"and you'll see how easy an ABCO is to start. *You can drive an ABCO, ladies.* EASY AS ABC!"

She flung out her arms and saw John Baxter standing, hands in pockets, staring at her. She flushed and turned away, vowing not to open her mouth again all evening. She saw her mother looking her most proper on one side of the velvet rope and Madame Butashky giving a talk on the other. Alberta was listening wide-eyed. Trudy hurried to her side.

Madame was saying, ". . . a ticket on that train if you want one."

They were discussing the Howdy Special because Mrs. Philpot answered, "There are no facilities for women."

Madame sniffed. "That means they don't want you to see them drinking and carousing."

Trudy groaned. That was just what her mother had suspected. She'd probably refuse to let Trudy race.

But Mrs. Philpot stiffened her back and said, "All the more reason ladies"—the word was emphasized only slightly but significantly—"should avoid the spectacle."

"Then why not form your own train? There must be other women in San Julio who want to see the end of the race. I'd organize it myself but the Academy requires my presence. Good evening, Trudy. A most illuminating talk. You persuaded me to purchase an ABCO. What about you, Millicent?"

Trudy noticed Miss Dupree hovering at Madame's other side, looking flustered and embarrassed.

Trudy said, "How would people know Miss Dupree was attending a social function if they didn't see her electric parked in front? It's her literary trademark, so to speak."

"Why, thank you, Trudence." Miss Dupree's flush was one of pleasure. She handed Trudy a pint jar filled with something pink. "This is for your hands."

"Miss Peterson mixed it in the Science Hall," said Madame

"From Marie Antoinette's own recipe," said Miss Dupree. "Miss Timson at the drugstore informed me of your difficulty, Trudence, so when the queen answered my psychophone I took the liberty of asking her advice. She says she wore this to bed at night under gloves."

"That explains her problem with King Louis," said Madame.

Miss Dupree turned crimson.

"What problem?" asked Alberta.

"You wouldn't understand," murmured Mrs. Philpot.

Madame gave an unladylike snort.

Trudy was astonished. It hadn't occurred to her that history could have ***s, too. Her mother's sharp "Trudence" reminded her to thank the ladies and send a message of gratitude to Miss Peterson. She was bursting to talk with Alberta but had no chance, not even on the telephone after they were home. Mrs. Philpot insisted they needed their rest.

Trudy went to bed but was too excited to sleep. She heard Quentin and John come home, but she couldn't wander around the hall with her hair tied in rags and her hands in her mother's old gloves. She punched the pillow into a firm ball and wondered why things never worked out right.

In the morning her hair was wavy, her hands smoother and the ground covered with snow.

FIVE

Quentin fretted and fumed about Alberta having to drive in snow, but Trudy thought half his worry was for himself. He had to meet Fred at dawn to drive the new tourer from the dealership to the Civic Hall and reload the spare wheels and emergency equipment into the racing ABCO. John Baxter had asked to walk with Trudy and Alberta.

"Maybe you can get them there before the race," Quentin told him as he left, halfway through a very early breakfast.

Trudy made a face at him which her mother couldn't see. Mrs. Philpot was insisting that everybody wear rubber overshoes and had gone next door to borrow a pair for John. She promised to take them back from Trudy and Alberta at the starting line.

Alberta arrived wearing not only overshoes but her red velvet jacket and the fur hat and muff her father had brought from San Francisco. She looked like an illustration from *McClure's* Christmas issue. Trudy trudged along at John's other side in an old knit cap and too-short skirt and wished she hadn't been so practical when she dressed.

Her mother had been right about the overshoes. The snow melted in their footsteps and left dark ribbons behind passing wagons. In front of the Civic Hall it had been tramped to puddles and ridges of dark slush. Trudy had a moment of panic, wondering if they'd missed the race after all. Surely trading a few snowballs with John hadn't taken that much time. It was barely light!

Then George Doty shouted, "Gangway!" and trotted past with a teakettle in each hand. Gregory Sr. followed with a milk pail full of steaming water.

"They should have worn overshoes," Alberta said.

John laughed. "They aren't soaking their feet. They're trying to start cold engines. I doubt if the race will start on time."

"At least it won't be our fault," said Trudy.

That didn't stop Quentin from complaining that they hadn't arrived sooner. Fred had refused to reload until Trudy was there to see what went where.

"Where is he?" said Alberta, and was concerned when she heard he was in the back alley guarding the equipment. "He'll catch pneumonia!"

"It's probably warmer out there than in here," Quentin told her, and went to start the unloading. John went with him.

It did seem colder inside the Hall, maybe because Trudy and Alberta had nothing to do. The committee members and newspapermen didn't seem uncomfortable, and some of the mechanicians had removed their coats. Quentin and Fred, lugging wheels and gear, had beads of sweat on their foreheads. But when Trudy climbed into the ABCO's front seat to supervise the loading, she could feel Alberta shaking. Trudy was shivering, too, and it got worse as the rear seat of the ABCO filled.

Besides the two spare wheels there were canvas strips, block and tackle, a coil of wire and numerous tools and spare parts. Then Mr. Philpot brought a water bag, a food hamper packed by Bertha and Mrs. Philpot and two carpetbags crammed with clothes and personal necessities. The other drivers turned to watch and grin. The weight was beginning to worry Trudy, too, but she cheerfully assured the newspapermen that weight didn't matter much to an ABCO.

While she and Alberta posed for photographers, two of the gasoline engines started. The noise was dreadful and the smell got worse, even with the Hall's front and rear doors propped open. One by one the other engines sputtered and roared.

Fred dug two packs of chewing gum from his pocket and handed them to Trudy. "Almost forgot. And remember, if you have to change a wheel, leave it. You can't spare the time and weight *will* make a difference."

"I know," Trudy assured him.

He reached up to shake her hand. "You'd make a fair mechanician if you wasn't such a lady."

Trudy stared open-mouthed as he walked around the ABCO to shake Alberta's hand. She didn't hear what he told her because Mr. Cunningham was handing her a packet of maps and directions. Then everybody was shaking hands, wishing luck or shouting instructions.

"Trudy!" Her father stepped onto the running board to hug and kiss her. His face had an expression she hadn't seen since James had had diphtheria. "Be careful now."

Trudy blinked and nodded, unable to speak for fear her teeth would chatter. Alberta was having trouble getting the muff's leather loop off her wrist. The fur barrel jumped in her hands as if alive. She caught it, shoved it into Trudy's lap and reached for the throttle. Her hand was shaking.

Slowly they followed the Gregorys' Model out the rear door. The sun shone in the alley. The snow had melted, leaving an inch of slippery mud. The Model skidded turning into First Street. Trudy gripped the wind-screen but Alberta made the turn without mishap, also the next one onto Main Street. And there they all were in front of the Civic Hall: her father looking proud and pleased now, Mr. Cunningham waving his derby, Quentin, John and Fred laughing and waving and all of them dodging through the crowd to stay even with the ABCO.

Trudy had never seen so many people in one place, not even when the circus came to San Julio. Nor so many policemen. They could hardly keep the crowd from the automobiles even before they reached the courthouse. The entire Academy was leaning over the curb, screaming and waving and throwing bits of colored paper, even Suzanne Davenport.

"There's Mama and Bertha!" Trudy stood to wave and blow kisses. "Look, Alberta!"

"*I'm driving!*" But even after they stopped between the Gregorys' Model and Mr. Nolan's Stoddard-Dayton, Alberta sat gripping the wheel and staring straight ahead. Trudy hoped the newspapermen would call her expression "intent and earnest" instead of "frightened."

She tried to distract them both by picking out familiar faces. "There's Miss Dupree. And Miss Timpkin!" She waved to them all and to everyone else who waved or shouted to her.

Mayor Gurke had been making a speech, but with the shouting and the gasoline engines, nobody could hear. Stubby O'Dell drew the mayor down to the starting line, handed him a watch and a green flag. The crowd hushed when Stubby waved the Ford forward. As it moved to the starting line, George Doty turned to wave at Trudy and Alberta.

"We'll be waiting for you in Yuma," he called. "Providing you get there tonight."

People laughed. Trudy kicked Alberta's ankle and muttered, "Smile." What Alberta managed was more of a grimace but nobody noticed. The mayor had dropped the flag and the crowd was cheering the Ford and its bicycle police escort down Main Street. Stubby waved ex-Councilman Very's Continental to the line.

After the argument about order in the procession, the dealers had drawn lots for starting positions and were leaving at five-minute intervals. But it seemed only seconds until the Gregorys' Model was waved to the line. The ABCO would be next.

Trudy's knees suddenly weakened and she sat down hard. Her mother had stopped waving her handkerchief and was wringing it. Mr. Philpot looked worried again and Mr. Cunningham was frowning at the sidewalk. Quentin, unable to pace in the crowd, was bobbing up and down. John and Fred looked almost as worried as Mr. Philpot. Trudy's stomach didn't feel right. She breathed deeply to settle it.

The crowd murmured and she noticed Stubby O'Dell waving impatiently.

"Alberta!" She kicked her again.

Alberta swallowed hard and reached a trembling hand for the throttle. She surprised Trudy with an uneven start and a sudden stop in front of the mayor. The crowd mistook it for eagerness or flamboyance and went wild. Academy students broke through the police line, and confetti piled up on the ABCO deep as the morning's snow. Everybody was yelling something: Trudy's parents, Mr. Cunningham, Miss Dupree and even Quentin. Trudy hoped none of the messages was important; she couldn't hear a word.

The race committee joined the police and cleared a passage just as the green flag swooped down. The ABCO rolled forward, smoothly this time, leaving a trail of streamers and confetti. Returning police escorts kept children from stepping off the curbs and bicyclists from getting too close. People were watching from porches or upstairs windows. Alberta kept the throttle open and they swept past the lumber mill and into ranch country.

"Yahoooooooo!" yelled Trudy, then "Damnation!"

SIX

"What's the matter?" Alberta sounded alarmed.

"Just that we still have your hat and muff. And the overshoes."

That must have been what her mother and Quentin had been trying to tell her.

Alberta said, "Don't worry. They don't weigh very much."

Not by themselves, but they'd said the same thing about Marie Antoinette's hand cream and the food hamper and half a dozen other things. Trudy sighed. At least the hamper would get lighter as they traveled. And as long as she had the muff, she might as well use it. Her fingers found the chewing gum and the packet Mr. Cunningham had given her. She unwrapped two sticks of gum, one for Alberta.

"No, thank you," said Alberta.

"We have to, in case we spring a leak. Chewing gum under friction tape will last forever."

"Can't we wait until we get a leak?"

"No time."

Alberta made a face but folded the stick of gum into her mouth. Trudy opened the packet.

"Here's a note!"

The road was still familiar. Alberta risked a look and gave a disappointed "Oh." It couldn't be from Fred. The stationery was lavender and the script formal.

"Miss Dupree," Trudy told her. "She wishes us winged victory and says Lucrezia Borgia is concerned about us. It's a good thing Mama packed that hamper."

"Don't laugh," said Alberta. "She was right about the snow."

"I thought you decided that meant my lily-white hands?"

"And that's another thing. That lotion works, doesn't it?"

"It's probably an old family recipe Miss Dupree forgot she remembered."

The road followed Alpine Creek past orchards and clearings. Horses, frightened to the far side of pastures, stared at the ABCO and began to move back toward the road.

Trudy laughed. "They're due for a shock when the Stoddard-Dayton comes by."

Two miles took them past the last of the ranches. The road left the creek and started down the mountain through tall pines. The pines thinned. They began to hear an engine and once, turning a curve, they saw the last of the Model's dust settling ahead of them. The curves sharpened and only scrubby lilac-flowered bushes separated the road from a steep drop.

Alberta pressed the brake and steered close to the opposite side where an even steeper slope rose above them. The road was littered with fallen rock. Alberta adjusted the throttle, slowing even more when the road narrowed and the turns became sharp as hairpins. In twenty minutes the Stoddard-Dayton caught up. Mr. Nolan blew the horn, oogah-ooogah!

Alberta carefully and slowly avoided a rock fall.

Ooogah-oooogah!

Trudy couldn't much blame him. She opened the map Mr. Cunningham had provided and traced the winding road.

"Alberta, it is another fourteen miles to the bottom. At this speed, we won't reach it until two o'clock and we'll still have a hundred and thirty miles to Yuma. We won't get there until the middle of the night!"

"We won't get to Yuma at all if we go over the side here."

Trudy kept her voice reasonable. "Alberta, the Butterfield stagecoaches came down this road."

"Not at full gallop."

She steered close enough to the side to scrape bushes, but just as Mr. Nolan started to pass, Alberta swerved to straddle a huge rock.

Oooogah! Oooogah!

They crept down into warm air. Trudy tugged off her jacket and helped Alberta off with hers. Alberta slowed the ABCO almost to a stop in the process.

OOOOGAH! OOOOGAH!

"That is extremely rude," said Alberta. She pulled off

the fur hat and, without looking, handed it to Trudy. "There are sun hats in my carpetbag and scarves to tie them with."

"Alberta!"

"You don't want to freckle, do you?"

"I don't want Mr. Nolan and his mechanician telling everyone we lost the race because we were changing into our automobiling costumes."

"We don't have to win this race, Trudy."

"Maybe not, but it won't do your father's dealership much good if we come in last."

"If I didn't have to squint so hard, maybe I could see better."

Trudy knew she was being blackmailed, but she knelt on the seat so she could reach Alberta's carpetbag. Mr. Nolan and his mechanician waved and shouted at her. She smiled and waved back. And burst out laughing at their expressions.

The hats weren't the fashionable ones from the Bon Ton. They were plain cheap straw, the wide brims broken from being packed. Trudy tried to put those parts at the sides where the scarves, laid over the crown and tied under the chin, would hide them. Alberta wouldn't turn her eyes from the road so Trudy had to tie her scarf under her ear. It looked interesting. She tied her own that way and turned to pack fur hat and muff in the carpetbag.

OOOOOGAH! OOOOOGAH! This time the cursing could be heard over the engine.

Alberta increased speed enough to raise a dust cloud.

The Stoddard-Dayton dropped back. The slope on the outside became less steep and Alberta opened the throttle still more. They came off the mountain at full speed, swept across the floor of a canyon and skidded on a turn at the opposite side. The dust cloud was spectacular. They drove out of it coughing and blinking and on a straight uphill road.

This side of the canyon was much lower than the opposite one. The road didn't wind but climbed diagonally across it. Trudy had a clear view.

"You can see everything, Alberta! There's the Stoddard-Dayton. Look!"

"I don't want to look!"

The drop-off was sheer cliff. Alberta hunched over the wheel chewing her gum furiously, the very thing she and Mrs. Philpot deplored. Trudy considered offering to drive, but stopping would take precious time. Besides, Alberta's fear was pushing her to reach the top in a hurry. Trudy watched the Stoddard-Dayton and its following billow of dust. It didn't drop back but hadn't gained any, either, by the time the ABCO crested the top and found gently sloping land broken only by widely scattered peaks.

Alberta gave a shaky sigh and wiped her forehead with her sleeve. "I hope that's the last cliff."

The map showed three sections of mountain road, but that was tomorrow and maybe the road would run between the mountains instead of up their sides. Trudy didn't mention them to Alberta.

"We need some luncheon," she said instead.

The road was straight but rough with potholes and bumps. They stuck their chewing gum on the windscreen and jounced and lurched along munching fried chicken legs, oatmeal cookies and wrinkled apples washed down with warm water that tasted of the canvas bag. After they'd eaten, their stale gum tasted peculiar. They threw it away and Trudy unwrapped fresh sticks.

Alberta pointed hers at the road. "Isn't that dust?"

"The Model!" said Trudy.

They grinned at each other. Trudy refilled their tin cups and they clinked them before drinking. When Trudy turned to repack the hamper, she saw a dust cloud behind them.

"Mr. Nolan's out of the canyon," she told Alberta.

Her feet were hot. She pried off her overshoes. After a long struggle and a few painful bruises, she managed to get Alberta's off, too. When she dropped them behind the seat, the Stoddard-Dayton was closer. The dust plume ahead seemed farther away.

"Alberta, are we slowing?"

She nodded. "I have to answer a call of nature."

"*Now?*"

"Of course now! I wouldn't be stopping if it wasn't now, would I?"

"Then stop and get it done. Don't creep along like this."

"I have to let Mr. Nolan pass."

"Alberta, this is a race. We are supposed to pass other automobiles, not let them pass us."

"But there aren't any bushes!"

There were, but they looked like loose bunches of buggy whips. The cactus grew only knee-high and the plants, like the rocky peaks, were carefully spaced, as if planted by a giant.

Trudy groaned and slumped in her seat. Alberta not only let Mr. Nolan pass, smothering them in white alkali dust, but she dawdled until the Stoddard-Dayton was far enough ahead to protect her modesty in case the men looked back.

"I'll go, too, so maybe we can avoid another stop." She gave Alberta a meaningful look that was wasted. Alberta was already picking her way around dusty clumps of yellow flowers. Trudy climbed down, surprised at how stiff she was, and followed.

Alberta turned and grabbed her arms. "Trudy! I just scared a lizard. This big." She held her hands eighteen inches apart.

"It won't hurt you. Hurry up!"

"But I swallowed my gum!"

Trudy hiked up her skirts. "We have plenty."

"But my insides will stick together!"

It took half an hour to convince Alberta she wasn't going to die. By then they were past the largest of the rocky peaks and the road had gotten worse. In some places the ruts were filled with drifted sand. In others ditches had been washed across the road, though Trudy found it hard to imagine rain in this land. Red flags tacked to stakes warned of the worst hazards but there were plenty of smaller holes and washes, and with the sun overhead, they cast no shadows and were almost impossible to see. The ABCO jounced and jolted over them or, when Alberta saw them in time to swerve, slewed and skidded and tossed Trudy around. After an hour of it, she felt like a well-beaten rug but she didn't dare complain, not when Alberta was grimly trying to make up the lost time.

Trudy braced herself and concentrated on watching for the Stoddard-Dayton's dust cloud and listening for escaping air. She didn't think Alberta would know if they got a flat tire.

From time to time she doled out their drinking water. Neither of them could remember being so thirsty. Trudy considered saving the water for the ABCO. They'd spent more time coming down the mountain than Mr. Cunningham had on his inspection tour. But Alberta thought they'd have enough steam to reach the first checkpoint if the road didn't do anything unusual.

The desert looked flat but wasn't, an illusion that must have killed a lot of pioneers. There were unexpected dips that could hide whole bands of Indians. They found the Stoddard-Dayton in one, nose down in a ditch cut by flash floods. Alberta had to swerve off the road to avoid hitting it.

"Keep going," Trudy told her.

Mr. Nolan and his mechanician had been sitting in the automobile's thin strip of shade, so whatever was wrong couldn't be fixed here. The men scrambled to their feet and watched the ABCO jounce along the top of the dip as Alberta searched for a safe place to cross.

Trudy knelt on the seat and yelled back, "What do

you need?" She hoped it wasn't water. Their bag was almost empty, and just thinking about it made her thirsty again.

The mechanician called, "Steering arm."

There was a spare in the rear seat of the ABCO, but it wouldn't fit the Stoddard-Dayton.

"We'll send the wagon," Trudy told him.

Mr. Nolan waved and nodded. Trudy got turned around and seated before Alberta crossed the dip. The bottom showed marks of other wheels. Alberta frowned, choosing her route back to the road. Trudy waited to be reminded that if they hadn't stopped to go to the toilet, the ABCO would be out of the race instead of the Stoddard-Dayton.

But Alberta said, "Trudy, there wasn't any flag."

"Are you sure?"

"Of course I'm sure!"

"One of the automobiles must have knocked it over when it turned off the road."

"I'd still have seen it."

"Maybe not." Alberta only took her eyes off the road to look at the gauges. Still, in this country, a square of red cloth was hard to hide. "Maybe it blew away."

Alberta shook her head. "George Doty took it."

Trudy was so surprised she forgot to wave again to Mr. Nolan when the ABCO lurched back onto the road, which didn't seem as smooth as the raw desert had been. She didn't bother to argue that the Gregorys were ahead of them. The Gregorys could have passed the Ford long ago.

"George wouldn't do anything like that," she said.

Alberta's tone said he would. "He's a nasty little boy."

Trudy grinned. "Not so little any more." But if getting mad at George Doty made Alberta drive like a real racer, Trudy wasn't going to argue. She clenched her teeth and held on.

"How far to the checkpoint?"

Trudy tried to remember. With the rough road and their present speed, she couldn't read the map.

"A mile past that peak." The road sloped up to circle its base. "Will we make it?"

"If it's downhill on the other side."

It was. But the ABCO ran out of steam and coasted to a stop two hundred yards from the old stagecoach station. A man in shirt sleeves, an unbuttoned vest and a wide-brimmed felt hat brought a pair of mules to pull them into the station yard.

"Save you having to tote," he said. "What's the name of this machine?"

Alberta told him, and he went to write it on a board propped against the station's mud brick wall. Then he led the mules around the building. Trudy and Alberta scrambled down and started flipping open hood latches. The brass was hot enough to burn, and Alberta yelped.

"Use the hem of your dress," Trudy told her.

"Not when we have to lift the hood off!"

Alberta climbed up and rummaged in the carpetbags for their gloves. Trudy went around the ABCO and flipped the latches on Alberta's side. When the hood was safely on the ground, they hurried to read the list on the board. No times were given, just positions when leaving the checkpoint.

"You were right about the flag," said Trudy, "only it wasn't George Doty who took it."

Ex-Councilman Very's Continental was ahead of them now. The Gregorys had passed it before reaching the checkpoint.

Trudy and Alberta trotted to the shelter, a canvas roof on four poles that shaded the rectangular five-gallon cans. If they'd once been neatly stacked, they weren't now. Only those marked NOLAN and CUNNINGHAM were still clustered together. Trudy unscrewed tops and sniffed, separating the cans with water from those holding gasoline.

"This one's water." She gave it to Alberta and found another for herself. "What's the matter?"

"I don't think we should drink this. It tastes funny."

"Minerals."

"Or poison. Remember Miss Dupree's note?"

Trudy nodded, studying the cans in front of her. She lifted the heavy can awkwardly and took a long drink. She couldn't decide which was worse, the warm temperature or the chemical taste. She crouched, poured water into her hand and splashed it over her face and the back of her neck. Warm as it was, it evaporated quickly and cooled her. Alberta watched her with awe and expectation.

"I guess Lucrezia Borgia was wrong." If she was disappointed, she was polite enough to keep it from her voice.

"Maybe not," Trudy told her. "We'll use Mr. Nolan's gasoline."

He wouldn't be needing it, and it was easier and safer to tamper with gasoline than drinking water. A few handfuls of sand in any one of the gasoline cans would put the ABCO out of the race.

The man brought the mules back hitched to a wagon. He leaned against it, rolling a cigarette and watching Trudy and Alberta trot back and forth between the shelter and the ABCO. They double-checked, sniffing each can before pouring. Trudy filled the gasoline tank, turned on the burner, checked it and the pilot light and went to help Alberta fill the boiler. By the time they stopped getting in each other's way, they were finished. Alberta climbed up to check the gauges.

"Toss down the water bag," Trudy told her.

Alberta shook her head, not taking her eyes off the dials. "You can drink that water if you want to, but I'll use what's left in the water bag."

"There isn't enough. You'll die of thirst." Exactly the fate that had worried her mother.

"I can manage until the next checkpoint."

They'd already wasted more time than a flat tire would have taken. Trudy dumped half the water from one of Mr. Nolan's cans to save weight and wedged the half empty can in the rear of the ABCO. The man was in his wagon, ready to go for Mr. Nolan and his mechanician.

Trudy waved. "Thank you!"

The man touched his hat brim but didn't start the mules until the ABCO pulled away. Alberta was back to her competent but noncompetitive driving. There was plenty of canned water in case she changed her mind about drinking it, but Trudy considered faking a stomach ache. If Alberta got thirsty enough, they might pass the Continental.

Some of the checkpoint wells were less bitter than others but none of them was sweet. The place with the foulest water called itself Mineral Wells on a sign over the gate and provided room and board for people who thought the water was a cure-all. It was the most prosperous of the old stagecoach stations. Some were shabby ranch houses, others just roofless shells. But, as Mr. Philpot had assured Trudy's mother, all had ready supplies of gasoline and water and a wagon to search for automobiles overdue long enough to cause worry. But the checkpoints and worry wagons wouldn't have comforted Mrs. Philpot if she'd seen the country around them.

Every time the road circled a peak or passed between two, it led to land lower, warmer and more barren. They drove two hours across alkali flats, throwing up a fine white dust that irritated eyes and skin.

Mr. Cunningham had provided goggles. Alberta thought they were ugly but she didn't object when Trudy got them out. It meant removing the hats and Trudy retied the scarves unevenly so they could tuck the long ends across their faces like Arabs. While she was kneeling, stretching to tie Alberta's goggles and scarf, Alberta hit two deep holes and almost ran off the road, which caused a good deal of yelling about whose fault it was.

Alberta had become less careful in her driving. She still believed Miss Dupree's warning and wanted to reach civilization before one of them collapsed. She kept sneaking worried looks at Trudy and asking every two miles how she felt, since Trudy was drinking the canned water freely and would show symptoms first. Alberta just sipped or rinsed her mouth and spat water over the side until Trudy told her she was losing too much chewing gum. She was in such a hurry she decided to drive past a checkpoint.

"We have enough fuel and water to reach the next one," she told Trudy.

She blew the horn as they approached, and Trudy cupped her hands and yelled, "Cunningham's ABCO! The Stoddard-Dayton is out of the race," to the young man who came out to watch. He just stared. Trudy turned and yelled again and he raised an arm.

Trudy sat back and worried. Mr. Cunningham's map wasn't as detailed as it could have been. But at the speed Alberta was driving, they should pass somebody. Not that she'd feel any safer with ex-Councilman Very behind them. But she kept raising her goggles to search for a dust cloud. When she saw one, they were out of the alkali flats and had refueled and watered. Trudy raised her arms and cheered.

They overtook it easily. It was raised by a buckboard moving away from the road, following a track so faint Trudy could hardly see it to a place she couldn't see at all. She'd always thought Gainesville a lonely place, with no railroad or telephones. But she shivered as she watched the buckboard.

Alberta noticed. "Does it hurt? Do you feel faint?"

"I feel fine."

But Alberta thought she was being noble. She opened the throttle still more and checked the gauges. "We'll skip the next checkpoint, too."

SEVEN

They passed the Model a mile before Brawley. Three boys were trying to help the Gregorys change a tire. Alberta gave a warning squeeze on the horn.

"Hey! There's another one," yelled one of the boys.

They all jumped for their bicycles. Gregory Jr. picked up a wrench one of them dropped. He nodded and waved at the ABCO.

Trudy frowned. She and Alberta had developed a routine, as precise as a square dance, for checkpoints. Well-wishing helpers would get in the way and slow them. They'd need every minute to stay ahead of the Model.

Somebody must have been watching for them. Or for the Model. The main street was lined with people waiting for them to pass. They waved and cheered, and their shouts all sounded encouraging. More boys ran or rode bicycles alongside the ABCO, casting envious looks at the goggles Trudy and Alberta had quickly pulled down to dangle around their necks. But they didn't think much of the ABCO.

81

"Can't be much of an automobile," said one. "It don't make any noise."

Alberta glared. Trudy pretended not to hear. She waved to people and watched for a restaurant. King Neptune's Cafe ("119 Feet Below Sea Level") didn't look any more appetizing than the chicken and potato salad she'd thrown overboard when they started to smell peculiar. There were still plenty of apples and cookies. But the apples were soft and spotted and the cookies made them thirsty. Alberta wouldn't eat any until they found safe water.

A young woman dodged the boys and bicycles to hand Trudy a half gallon jar. She trotted beside the ABCO. "Buttermilk. It's fresh."

It was also cool. Trudy could hardly believe it. "Thank you! Oh, thank you!"

"I thought buttermilk would do you the most good. If I knew anything else to help, I'd do it." She was falling behind. She called, "We want you to win!"

Trudy leaned out and thanked her again.

"She's a suffragette," said the boy who didn't like the ABCO. He made it sound like a warning against drinking the buttermilk.

Trudy groped for cups, found she was sitting on one and raised up to pull it out.

"Are you one?" said the boy.

"One what?"

"Suffragette."

"I'm a mechanician."

"Honest Injun?"

Trudy crossed her heart and held up her hand, palm out. She wished they could drink the buttermilk now while it was cool, but they were almost to the checkpoint, a livery stable at the east end of Brawley. She asked the boy his name (it was Harold), then if there was some place they could buy sandwiches.

"Sure." He wheeled his bicycle away without waiting for money.

The familiar canvas shelter wasn't in the livery-stable yard but some distance beyond, probably because of the danger of fire. Trudy had been counting on the stable's fence to keep the crowd away. Half the town was following them. Five men waited at the shelter. They came forward offering help even before Alberta stopped the ABCO.

Trudy assigned two to remove the hood. They were as slow as she and Alberta had been at first and they put it down in Alberta's way so that Trudy had to ask them to move it. But it gave them a chance to drink some buttermilk while it was still cool. Alberta drank three cups. Trudy couldn't find the other cup and drank from the jar, much to the horror and delight of the onlookers.

Alberta sighed. "Oh, that's good."

Trudy replaced the lid and set the jar on the floor. She handed the water bag to one of the gaping men. "Would you fill that, please? The rest of you can keep those people away. No, thank you, we can manage the rest better by ourselves."

When she jumped down, she had to grab the side of the ABCO to keep from falling. At every stop she was stiffer and took longer to loosen. Alberta let one of the men help her down and to the shelter. Trudy hobbled past her, glaring. They were soon moving briskly in the familiar pattern and ignoring the usual questions about why they were using Mr. Nolan's cans. They had the hood on and the latches fastened before the men could move to help.

An engine sounded in town. Trudy climbed up, checked the water bag and held the buttermilk jar on her lap. It was no longer cool, but still precious.

The crowd milled back and forth, torn between watching the arrival of the Model and the departure of the ABCO. Alberta muttered as she tried to steer them through.

"Hey!" Harold pedaled up and threw Trudy a package in butcher's wrap, fortunately tied with string.

Trudy earned a grin by catching it one-handed. "How much?"

"Nothing. My ma made them. And she's no suffragette."

"She's a kind and generous lady with a noble son."

Alberta humphed.

Harold flushed and ducked his head. Then he stood on the pedals and called, "I'll race you!"

The bicycle got through the crowd easier than the ABCO, but once on empty road Alberta opened the throttle wide and left the bicycle in a cloud of dust. Harold didn't seem to resent it. When Trudy looked back, he had one foot on the ground and was waving his whole arm.

"That'll teach him about ABCOs," said Alberta.

"It'll make him think you're a suffragette." Trudy untied the package and found thick roast beef sandwiches. "God bless Harold's mother!"

"And the unknown suffragette," added Alberta. "May I have another drink?"

"If you promise not to slow down."

The road wouldn't let them continue at top speed, but Alberta kept their small lead on the Model. They ate and drank. Trudy saved the rest of the buttermilk for Alberta. And they sang "In My Merry Oldsmobile," making up words that fit their situation, until they reached Mammoth Wash and got stuck in the sand.

When Trudy got out with the shovel, she sank to her ankles in reddish sand. She dug out the wheels and laid down the canvas strips for traction, then almost had to dig the strips out after Alberta drove over them. When digging and the canvas strips didn't help, they had to wait for one of the teams of horses hired for this stretch of road. Trudy was so tired and gritty she hardly cared when the lighter Model passed them.

There were no big drifts or sand holes after Mammoth Station, but the road faded to ruts. Eighteen miles north of the Yuma crossing, the sun set. Trudy lit the carbide lamp. It had to be aimed by hand and it jounced back and forth over the ruts. They were tired and short-tempered and were soon blaming each other. Trudy wondered how the other mechanicians worked gasoline pressure pumps at the same time.

They crept along, jerking ahead, then slowing, for

nearly an hour until somebody shouted, "Stop! Wait!" Alberta braked to a halt, then inched forward until the light showed Gregory Jr. standing in the ruts, shading his eyes with one hand. The Model's lamp had quit, and the automobile was creeping along even more slowly than the ABCO.

"Didn't want you to hit us," young Gregory told them.

They let him ride as far as the Model on the running board, and Trudy gave him apples and cookies.

Alberta called to Gregory Sr. as they passed, jouncing over rough ground, "You can follow us to the Yuma crossing."

"If you can keep up," Trudy added and gave Alberta a nudge. "Let's go."

"Watch where you're swinging that light."

"I can't help it. Get back on the road."

The light caught a startled rabbit, then they were back in the ruts.

Alberta said, "We can't just drive off and abandon them."

"They aren't stuck. They were doing just fine before we caught up. Do you want to start off tomorrow with that automobile goosing us?"

Alberta giggled and kept going, increasing speed dangerously when they saw the lights of the ferry landing. There were three times as many lights on the opposite side of the river. Trudy turned off the carbide lamp while Alberta maneuvered onto the ferry. Indians ran it. They stared at the ABCO and murmured among themselves.

Trudy said, "Want to get out and stretch?"

Alberta shook her head. "I might not get back up."

They took off hats and goggles, smoothed their hair and dabbed their faces with the last of the water. Then there was nothing to do but watch the Arizona shore approach.

One of the Indians said softly, "Why doesn't this one make a noise?"

"It's a steam engine," Trudy told him.

"Like the train?"

"That's right." By the time she'd explained the advantages of an ABCO, she could hear men shouting on the dock and make out individual faces in the torchlight.

"When you come back," said the Indian, "maybe I buy it."

"By God," somebody ashore yelled, "it's the girls! Where's Cunningham?"

Their fathers ran to the end of the dock, shouting and waving. Trudy and Alberta waved back. George Doty whooped and waved a beer mug. "Told you I'd be waiting for you, kiddos," he called. Stubby O'Dell led the Howdy Band in "Oh, You Beautiful Doll" until a torch fell on them, causing confusion and panic. The ferry nudged the dock. Two Indians jumped to tie it fast. Alberta reached for the throttle and edged the ABCO forward.

"Don't stop!" Quentin shouted, pushing a way clear. "Keep going. You have to check in."

He jogged ahead, clearing a way and pointing out a barn. Like a horse headed for its home stable, the ABCO tore up the slope and across the square, Alberta honking steadily at people and dogs.

"There!" Trudy pointed at the barnyard.

Lanterns lit the gate and the man, watch in hand, who was waiting to clock them in. As soon as they cleared the gate, Alberta stamped on the brake pedal. The ABCO skidded halfway around and stopped. Dust and debris swirled and settled.

"We made it," Alberta said softly.

"We surely did," said Trudy.

They looked at each other and grinned.

"Can't stay there." A man in Levis and boots waved them into the deserted barn. "Take everything you need. We're locking this up until starting time tomorrow."

They handed him their carpetbags, and he helped them down. They thanked him and trudged wearily across the barnyard, through the gate and into their fathers' arms. Quentin was there. Also John Baxter. Everyone hugged everybody and Trudy found she didn't feel quite so tired, though her legs vibrated as if she were still driving.

They crossed the square to the hotel, stopping several times to receive congratulations or good luck wishes. John had saved them a meal from the barbecue. He'd also ordered baths, but they postponed those. The Howdy Special was due to leave in a half hour, and their fathers had questions. They took turns eating and talking, with most of the crowd from the dock trying to listen.

Trudy told about the Stoddard-Dayton, the suffragette and Harold and his mother's sandwiches, the kind of things her father needed. She just wished the other newspapermen weren't there to hear, too. Alberta gave exaggerated details of the alkali flats and sand holes, delighting the newspapermen by making Trudy display her blistered hands. Neither of them mentioned Alberta's distrust of water (she'd decided Yuma's was safe and was drinking enough to founder a horse) or Trudy's use of Mr. Nolan's gasoline. Ex-Councilman Very was among the listeners, but if he was surprised to see them, he'd had time to hide it.

A boy ran through the lobby, yelled, "Ferry's coming!" through the dining room door and pounded out again. Everybody around the table stampeded back to the dock. Mr. Philpot smiled and gathered his notes.

"Just time to make the morning edition," he said, and stood to walk to the station. "I'll also telegraph your mother," he told Trudy, "so she can sleep tonight."

Trudy smiled and nodded. She guessed that he'd also telegraph his story to other newspapers besides the San Julio *Gazette*, beating the newspapermen who were waiting for the last entry to clock in.

"I better go get the time," said Quentin.

"Later," said Mr. Cunningham. "We have to plot strategy."

But when the Howdy Special blew its boarding whistle, the only advice they'd had was, "Hold your lead time." Which Quentin estimated to be about forty minutes. John Baxter had gone off to rearrange their baths. He and Mr. Philpot returned just in time to say good-by in the lobby. Their fathers didn't want Trudy and Alberta to go to the station, and they were so tired they only protested out of habit.

Trudy made Quentin stand guard outside the bathroom, which was downstairs and behind the kitchen. He argued that it wasn't necessary since the other teams were sleeping in a dormitory down the street.

"There are other people in this hotel," Trudy said. "And Mama said . . . ."

"All right!" He sat on the back stairs to watch the bathroom door, which Trudy carefully locked from inside. The copper tubs were undersize and the water had cooled, but next to passing the Model, it was the best thing that had happened all day. If the tubs had been large enough for them to scrunch down and rest their heads, they would probably have fallen asleep. When she pushed herself up and out, Trudy glanced over and thought she saw Alberta nodding. They had to wake Quentin so he could escort them up the stairs to their room.

"A fine chaperone he is," Trudy grumbled.

"He can't help it," said Alberta. "He's tired."

"*He's* tired?" Trudy ignored the hairbrush on the dresser. She was too tired to brush a hundred strokes, but she used Marie Antoinette's lotion on her hands. Her blisters had broken, and she wondered if she shouldn't wear the gloves tomorrow. Alberta slathered the lotion on her face as well as her hands.

"This race is ruining our complexions," she said.

The mirror was so crazed and the lamp chimney so dirty, Trudy didn't know how she could tell. But she asked Alberta to coat her face, too.

The straw mattress rustled at the slightest movement. It set them giggling, and Trudy wondered how they'd get any sleep. But suddenly she was locked in a haymow and John Baxter was trying to rescue her. Then she woke, and the sounds of rescue were just Quentin pounding on the door.

Alberta burrowed deeper in the mattress, the sound of the straw almost covering her groan. Trudy pushed herself up to sit on the edge of the bed. She stared at the scrap of worn rug and wondered what she was doing there.

"Wake up!" yelled Quentin and pounded harder. Trudy hobbled to the door, unlocked it and opened it to find Quentin naked except for his trousers, which he clutched with one hand. "Hurry," he told her. "The race has started!"

Trudy stared at him.

"Didn't you hear? *The race has started!* HURRY!"

Trudy slammed the door and reached for her clothes piled on a straight-backed chair. "Alberta, help me!"

The straw rustled. "What happened?"

"Quentin overslept." She pulled on her underwear and pushed her arms into her shirtwaist. Behind her, Alberta started on the bottom buttons while Trudy stepped into her petticoat, drew it up and buttoned it. "I'll get the ABCO started while you dress and pack."

"What about breakfast?" Alberta waited to fasten the top button until Trudy had pulled her skirt over her head. Then she went for a hairbrush.

Trudy buttoned her skirt, tugged it right side front and pushed her feet into her boots. They felt as tight as new ones, maybe because her feet were bare.

"Your stockings!" said Alberta.

"No time." She didn't take time to button up her boots, either. "Get something we can eat on the way. And get lots."

Alberta followed her to the door, trying to brush her hair. "Don't fuss," Trudy told her. "We'll be wearing those hats. And *hurry!*"

She wondered how close they were to their starting time. Quentin had forgotten to mention it. A lot of help he was, always asleep when they needed him. His open door showed a messy but unoccupied room. Trudy clumped down the front stairs.

Her boots were suddenly loose and awkward to walk in. She shuffle-flapped down the street, raising almost as much dust as an automobile. The timekeeper stood outside the barnyard gate. He nodded to Trudy and glanced at his watch.

She longed to ask how much time she had, but no matter how little, she couldn't hurry any faster and she wouldn't ask with so many people watching and listening. The Gregorys leaned against the inside of the fence talking to men lounging against the outside. The Model stood in the barnyard but the engine wasn't running. Not that it meant anything. The Gregorys had a forty-three minute wait after the ABCO was due to leave. There was no sign of the Ford or Continental, not even a dust cloud. Their leads were more than an hour.

"Morning," said Gregory Sr.

Gregory Jr. grinned. "Had your beauty sleep?"

There were other grins and some sniggers. Trudy clumped into the barn. The man who'd helped them the night before was still standing guard. He helped Trudy lift off the hood and carry cans. He chose those marked CUNNINGHAM and, after a moment's hesitation, Trudy accepted them. There was probably little risk, as well guarded as the barn had been, and asking for Mr. Nolan's would waste time in explanations. Refueling took longer than it did when she teamed with Alberta, but not nearly as long as if she'd had to do it herself. The bending and lifting loosened her aching muscles and made her stomach rumble.

When she drove the ABCO into the barnyard, the timekeeper, without raising his eyes from the watch, said, "I called five minutes two minutes ago."

Alberta and Quentin were just leaving the hotel, Quentin with the carpetbags and Alberta carrying baskets. They started to run. Trudy grabbed the water bag and jumped to the ground. She half lost a boot and almost fell. Her momentum carried her past the Gregorys to the watering trough. It looked as unused as the barn, but the pump had been primed. Water gushed out, soaking Trudy's sleeve and front before she finished filling the water bag. She galloped back and tossed it into the ABCO just as the timekeeper brought down his arm.

The onlookers burst into jeering cheers. Trudy flushed, hauled herself up and drove to meet Alberta. Quentin tossed bags and baskets into the rear and Alberta into the driver's seat. Trudy barely had time to crawl over and make room, but they'd lost four minutes of the lead. Quentin ran after them to tell them so.

"*You* lost four minutes," was the way he put it.

By the time Trudy thought of a suitable answer, they were almost out of town. She waited until they were safely past a team of rearing horses, then asked, "Did you bring anything to eat?"

Alberta nodded. "In the baskets. Quentin told the cook to pack whatever he had."

"It looks as if he just wrapped all his leftovers in tortillas."

There were some strange fillings besides the usual ones of meat and beans. There was also half an apple pie and two bottles of soda water with tops Trudy couldn't open. She muttered unflattering things about the intelligence of Quentin and the cook.

Alberta frowned. There was a ridge of mountains across their way. "Maybe we should telegraph Miss Dupree and ask if she's had any more messages."

Imitating Miss Dupree's precise voice, Trudy said, "Napoleon's Josephine wishes to remind you that racing teams travel on their stomachs." She examined two of the folded tortillas and asked in her own voice, "Which do you want, sauerkraut and sausage or creamed noodles?"

Neither tasted as awful as it looked. They shared the rest, then the last of Bertha's cookies. They agreed to save the pie for noon, but it was soon eaten, along with the rotting apples from the hamper. They weren't really hungry but eating was the only way to break the monotony.

Hour after hour they traveled the same sandy ground, sometimes strewn with pitted volcanic rocks, with the same scrubby bushes and yellow flowers and the same rocky peaks. Even the two mountain ridges outside Yuma had been dull, the road leading through canyons or over gently sloping shoulders. The only time they'd been high enough to see a dust plume miles ahead, the sun had been in their eyes. So they ate until the food was gone and then chewed gum. Racing was as unexciting as preparing for it had been.

Trudy didn't fall asleep but she wasn't always fully awake, either. Once Alberta drove toward the edge of the road, though her eyes were open and looking ahead as usual. Trudy yelled and grabbed the wheel, worried about their tires if they got into the cactus that had begun to appear among the dusty bushes.

Refueling was a welcome relief. It stretched cramped muscles and stirred their blood, though Trudy noticed they didn't move as quickly as they had the day before. They'd stopped using Mr. Nolan's gasoline. Trudy had decided that if ex-Councilman Very had tampered with the gasoline, he'd have figured out how they reached Yuma and would be watering the NOLAN cans now. It also saved arguments, though only a few men at the refueling stations kept close watch on what they did. They were too interested in the automobile.

The race boards always showed the Ford leading, then ex-Councilman Very. Alberta kept their lead on the Model because Trudy seldom saw any sign of it behind them.

They reached Gila Bend early in the afternoon. They'd decided to refuel for the last time in Buckeye, but slowed down as they entered Gila Bend so Trudy could give one of the boys in the usual welcoming committee money to get them sandwiches.

"I'll meet you at the bridge," he told them. "Deke'll show you the way."

Trudy didn't think they could get lost. Most of the town was on one street and the bridge was clearly marked on Mr. Cunningham's map. But he hadn't noted that it was a railroad bridge. Two rows of planks had been laid over the ties for automobiles' wheels. Between the planks and ties, the Gila River could be seen far below.

EIGHT

"**G**od help us!" Alberta went white and stopped the ABCO.

"I'll drive." Trudy jumped down and ran around to the driver's side.

Alberta stared at the bridge. "I can't cross that, driving or not."

"Yes, you can." Trudy climbed up and pushed at Alberta until she moved onto the other seat. "Just close your eyes. Put your goggles on."

They'd been wearing them ready around their necks. Trudy had to help adjust them. Alberta's hands were shaking.

"I can still see," she said.

"They're just to remind you to keep your eyes closed." Trudy really hoped they'd hide Alberta's closed eyes from onlookers. She'd have preferred blindfolding Alberta like a frightened horse but she didn't dare, not with most of Gila Bend waiting to see if they'd cross. Men at the opposite end of the bridge were staring at them. So were the boys they'd chased off the planks so the ABCO could cross.

The boy she'd given coins to skidded to a halt. Then he saw Trudy, went around and handed her the sandwiches. "What's the matter with her?" He nodded at Alberta.

"Too much sun," Trudy told him.

He nodded, wished Trudy luck and added, "Don't worry about trains. We're keeping watch for them."

Alberta made a strange noise.

"Think of something else," Trudy told her. "Something nice . . . the gala! You're at tonight's gala!" She pushed the map into Alberta's clenched hands. "Don't look! This is your dance program and it's completely filled."

Alberta smiled. Trudy glanced back, expecting to see the Model bearing down on them, but the road and sky were still clear. She started the ABCO forward.

"Trudy, I . . . ."

"*Eyes closed!* Think of your gown . . . you're coming down the Grand Stairway, into the ballroom. . . ." Trudy stood to see that the tires were aligned with the ends of the planks. "Your hair's *en pompadour* . . . with egret feathers. . . ." The planks looked as narrow as match sticks. The river below was in flood. Trudy's knees and elbows went weak. "You're dancing. . . ."

She sat down, reminded herself she'd wanted an exciting race and eased open the throttle. The thump of the planks made Alberta jump.

"Eyes closed!" Trudy was shouting in a whisper, like Quentin. She forced herself to smile across Alberta at staring Gila Benders. "The first dance is with your father . . . a waltz. . . . You open the gala. . . ." Which would mean they'd won the race which would mean they'd gotten over the bridge.

Trudy didn't think they would. She was terrified. She couldn't see over the hood to check on the wheels' position. She kept correcting for where she thought they were and guessed sooner or later she'd run them off the boards.

Another part of her mind was deciding the order of dancing partners for winners of the race. Suddenly she remembered something Quentin had told Alberta during the driving lessons. She forced herself to look up from the hood and aim the ABCO at the far ends of the planks. It seemed to work. At least she was holding the wheel steady, and the only noise was the steady thump-thud of the planks on the railroad ties.

She took a deep breath, released it slowly and went on. "Your next dance is with Quentin. . . ."

"John Baxter," said Alberta.

"But Que— All right!" She couldn't risk Alberta's opening her eyes to argue in the middle of the bridge. "The next dance is with John . . . a polka." Let her try romancing during that. She continued her sketchy narrative, borrowing from the stories they'd been reading, until she noticed the men at the end of the bridge. They looked as if they were paying off bets.

She glanced at Alberta but she was smiling, eyes closed, caught in her own vision of the gala. She probably hadn't changed partners since the polka with John. When they reached the end of the bridge, Trudy announced it with a shout of, *"We're over!"* and was pleased at the way it jerked Alberta out of her dream.

"Oh!" She relaxed. "We're over."

"That's what I said."

"I thought you meant we were *over*." She glanced back at the water and shivered.

As they bumped off the tracks, there were a few thin cheers, mostly from children. The man who'd collected the bets raised his hat. The rest glared. Alberta didn't notice. She was too busy heaping thanks on Trudy, which was embarrassing after the way Trudy had deliberately scared her.

Trudy stopped the ABCO and traded seats, hoping the strain of driving would quiet her. But the fear, or her relief from it, had loosened something in Alberta. She drove full speed, chattering and even turning to look at Trudy. The road was a good one, but the ABCO's rear end waggled alarmingly on curves.

Too much weight. But the only items they could positively spare were the carpetbags and the hamper. Trudy was still trying to think of a way to persuade Alberta to dump the carpetbags when they saw the trees that marked Buckeye.

Like Gila Bend, most of Buckeye was on one street. There was a crowd at the far end. Also a plume of dust.

"The Continental!" said Alberta.

Trudy leaned sideways to see around the dusty windscreen. "Can't be." They'd been going almost sixty but that wasn't enough to make up an hour's lead, or more. "It must be an accident. Or a runaway horse. Whoa!"

She directed Alberta into Marshal's Sand and Gravel Yard where the refueling station had been set up. It was deserted except for a girl about ten who was playing tightrope walker atop stacks of adobe bricks. They grated when she jumped off. She walked over to watch Trudy unlatch her side of the hood.

"Hello." Trudy took a second to stretch her shoulders back. "Where is everybody?"

The girl pointed to the end of town. "Seeing the other one off."

Trudy stared over the road. Alberta's smile said *I told you so.*

"We can pass him! We can be second!" said Trudy. "Come on!"

They wrestled the hood off for the last time and galloped to the canvas shelter. The girl followed, chanting, "I know something you don't know." Trudy ignored her until she smelled spilled gasoline. Alberta wrinkled her nose and backed away from the shelter.

Trudy turned to the girl. "What do you know?"

"Give me those and I'll tell you." She pointed to the goggles dangling from Trudy's neck.

"Tell me first."

The girl shook her head. Trudy untied the cords and held out the goggles but she didn't let go when the girl took them. They stared at each other until the girl said, "He poured out gasoline and put in water."

"Which cans?"

"All of them."

Alberta used one of Quentin's favorite words.

Trudy slumped to the ground. "Why didn't anyone see him?"

She didn't expect an answer, especially since she'd

released the goggles. But the girl, happily polishing the lenses with her skirt, said, "He took them over to the saloon. All 'cept me."

From her description, it had been ex-Councilman Very who'd done the dirty work while the mechanician stayed in the saloon entertaining. That's where the hour's lead had gone. Probably less. Trudy wasn't sure of the Continental's top speed but none of the automobiles could match the ABCO's pace from Gila Bend.

She looked up at Alberta. "It doesn't make sense."

Alberta wasn't listening. She wailed, "What are we going to do? We have to get to Phoenix. My entire life depends on it."

There wasn't likely to be gasoline in Buckeye. There was hardly any use for it. It was just a by-product of making kerosene.

"Kerosene!" Trudy scrambled to her feet and headed for the ABCO. "I can adjust the burner. Go get some kerosene."

But when they pooled their money they had six cents, a penny short even for a gallon of gasoline.

"Barter," said Trudy, rummaging in the rear seat for screwdriver and wrench. "Somebody here must want a fur muff."

"Trudence Philpot . . .!"

"My whole life depends on it," Trudy mimicked.

"But I only wore it this once!"

But while she protested and mourned, she found her carpetbag and lifted out the muff. The girl was watching them as if they were a new kind of minstrel show. Trudy prodded her with the wrench.

"Can you take Alberta to the general store?"

The girl nodded and led Alberta to the street. There were people on it now but nobody had yet noticed the ABCO. Trudy bent over the burner. It took only a minute to turn it off and adjust the holes larger. She was reopening the fuel line when somebody called, "Hey! Get away from that automobile!"

Trudy straightened and turned.

The man flushed and touched his hat brim. "Sorry, miss. I thought you were Amy. She's been hanging around here all day pestering folks."

"At least she was here," Trudy told him. "Which is more than I can say for the people who were supposed to help us."

"But we weren't expecting you. That is, not so soon. I mean, we were told . . . ."

He kept getting in the way trying to apologize. Other people noticed them. Trudy tossed the tools into the back seat and sprinted for the water cans.

"Just keep those people out of my way," she told the man, then set down the can she'd just lifted. Phoenix was only—she consulted the map in her pocket—thirty-four miles. If she put just enough water in the boiler to get them there, it would cut their weight considerably.

Wishing she had Alberta's help, she estimated the water and poured it into the boiler. By then Alberta was back with the kerosene, Amy officiously clearing a way through the onlookers. Alberta still had her muff, tucked up under her arm away from the oily cans.

Trudy wiped her forehead on her sleeve. "How did you get the kerosene?"

"Credit." She uncapped a can and poured it carefully. "I only got enough to get us to Phoenix and Mr. Pincer agreed a fur muff was gross overpayment."

"And you just smiled at him and he gave you credit?" Alberta always got what she wanted with a smile and a fluttery look. If Trudy had had any sense, she'd have kept quiet about using kerosene. They could have waited in Buckeye for rescue until the race was over and John Baxter on his way back to Boston. But then Trudy wouldn't have seen him again, either. She sighed and bent for the handles on her side of the hood.

As they heaved it up, Alberta said, "Amy put her goggles up for security." The hood clanked into place. Alberta grinned over it. "But only after I bought her a bag of candy."

Trudy glanced up from snapping latches. One side of Amy's face bulged grotesquely. From the size of the brown bag she held, the candy must have cost more than the kerosene.

"Daddy will send the money right away," Alberta told the girl. "You'll have your goggles back Monday." As they settled into their sun-hot seats, she muttered to Trudy, "Now we know why she needs them. She's planning to be a bandit—*what's that?*"

Opening the throttle had produced a shrieking whistle, a cross between a teakettle and a cat. It drew people like a fire engine.

"It's from burning kerosene," Trudy told her.

"Can't you do something?"

"I did. That's what causes the noise."

"You mean we're going to have this all the way to Phoenix?"

Trudy shrugged. If Fred had mentioned the noise stopping, Trudy hadn't been listening.

Then Alberta was too busy to complain. All the horses in hearing were trying to bolt. All along the street they reared and jerked at reins, eyes rolling with fright. People ran and yelled, mostly at Alberta. What they said was drowned by horses and the ABCO.

It was more frightening than crossing the railroad bridge. There the danger had been predictable and Trudy had had control. A runaway horse was as liable to charge the ABCO as run from it. But Alberta got them through town with only insults and one kick that bent a rear fender.

They were both giddy. When Trudy said shakily, "At least they'll know we're coming," they laughed uproariously for three miles. Then they sang a song they'd learned from a photographer but hadn't dared sing around home.

"There was I. B. Dam and U. B. Dam and the whole Dam family," they roared.

The ABCO shrilled along at top speed. Trudy had convinced Alberta that it made less noise with the throttle wide open. She watched the Continental's dust cloud grow closer. For a while she saw two clouds. When they settled to one, she blamed it on heat distortion. But during the seventh verse, they found the Ford stopped in the road.

Repairs had been made. Mr. Becker was in the driver's seat and George Doty was standing in front ready to turn the crank.

Alberta yelled, "That's why they call it a runabout. It runs about this far and stops!"

She laughed as she made a grand sweep off the road to pass. There was a bang! A tire, thought Trudy, until the ABCO swung back to the road and they saw George picking himself up off it. Alberta gasped.

"Don't stop," Trudy told her. From Fred's scornful comparisons with gasoline engines, she guessed what had happened though she didn't understand it. "He didn't wait for Mr. Becker to retard the spark. The engine backfired and the crank threw him."

"He'll probably blame me," said Alberta. "Is he hurt?"

With the ABCO whistling, Trudy couldn't tell if her tone was worried or hopeful. She turned to look. "No."

But there was something wrong with the Ford. It dropped slowly behind. No wonder ex-Councilman Very had gotten everyone out of the way so he could water the gasoline. He must have seen the Ford attempting repairs in Buckeye or heard about its trouble and knew he was first. It had been worth the delay to be sure nobody caught up, and with the risk he'd taken, he must have been sure that somebody could.

Trudy yahooed and punched Alberta's shoulder. *"We can win!"*

Alberta stared at her. Trudy explained. Alberta grinned and reached for the throttle, but it was already wide open. She hunched forward, urging the ABCO onward. They gained steadily on the Continental until they were catching its dust. Then it held its small lead. Trudy helped Alberta fix her goggles. "How far?"

Alberta's lips moved as she figured. "Eleven miles."

Trudy hitched up her skirt and climbed over her seat back. She almost fell out pushing the second spare wheel over the side. She flung wrenches, tire iron and screwdrivers after it. The dust got worse. Even with her back to it she had to squint. She didn't get the canvas strips out on the first heave. They dragged and slowed the ABCO a crucial few seconds. Bracing against the bounce and lurch of the ABCO, Trudy dragged ropes and tackle to the door opening and shoved them out. Shovels followed.

"Not the carpetbags!" screamed Alberta. She reached back and tried to pull one from Trudy's grip.

"Watch out!" Trudy hung on until Alberta got them back on the road. They'd narrowly missed an irrigation ditch.

"Not the carpetbags," Alberta repeated, but she kept her hands on the wheel and her goggles forward. "I already sacrificed my muff."

"You did not!"

"But I would have!"

True enough. "Then I'll just throw mine."

"NO!" This time she did turn.

So it was Marie Antoinette's lotion she wanted. Trudy smiled grimly. "If you don't pass, I'll have to throw them."

She tossed two unopened bottles of sarsaparilla and the water bag behind them and slid down into the foot space, her back against the front seats. Even looking backward, she couldn't open her eyes more than a crack. Trees and house roofs rushed past, then three- and four-story buildings. A gasoline engine drowned the ABCO's whistling. Trudy made blinkers of her hands and risked a look sideways.

They were passing the Continental! Beyond its rear deck she saw eager faces, then frightened faces turning and scattering, leaving a space suddenly filled with a wild-eyed horse. Trudy ducked her head and covered it with her arms. Both automobiles turned, but the smaller Continental turned faster and struck the ABCO's fender. The ABCO skidded, hit the Continental and sent it into a spin. Like a monstrous clumsy dance, the automobiles touched and turned, banging and crashing.

When the noise and movement stopped, Trudy lifted her head. She stared into a row of official-looking faces, some familiar, some strange, but all astonished. And all standing at a respectful distance. Then Trudy saw the tape, the finish tape, still unbroken a few yards behind the ABCO.

"Alberta!" She pulled herself to her knees. "*Reverse!*"

The Continental had already backed into a turn. Gears ground as ex-Councilman Very shifted forward. Trudy pounded Alberta on the back. "REVERSE!"

Alberta stomped on the pedal. The ABCO shot backward, breaking the tape and scattering officials.

"*We won!*" Trudy screamed and beat Alberta on the back again, this time in joy.

"*We won!*" Mr. Cunningham pushed through the running crowd, John Baxter at his heels.

Ex-Councilman Very stopped his Continental, its hood even with the ABCO's rear deck. He pawed aside a broken end of tape, stood on the seat and raised his clasped hands.

"The winner!" he shouted, and just as many people crowded around to congratulate him as clustered around Mr. Cunningham.

"The ABCO won!" Mr. Cunningham shouted back. "Easy as ABC!"

"Nobody can win a race going backward!"

"SHOW ME THE RULE...."

Then Trudy's father was grinning up at her and saying, "Have a statement for the press?"

"Papa!" She leaned down to hug him. "Where's Mama? And Bertha?"

"Up there." He pointed his cigar at the third-story window in the hotel half a block away. Trudy waved and blew a kiss. So did Alberta when she learned who was watching there.

The crowd around the ABCO burst into cheers and waved hats as the official decision was announced.

"We won!" yelled Alberta, shaking the ABCO as she jumped up and down.

Mr. Cunningham helped her down and into the rear beside Trudy. Then he took the driver's seat and started the ABCO slowly down the middle of the street. Newspapermen paced alongside, but they were more interested in congratulating Mr. Cunningham and asking his plans for the future than in hearing how Trudy and Alberta had won the race. Mr. Cunningham's invitation to help celebrate brought more cheers than the announcement of their victory. When they reached the hotel, everyone followed Mr. Cunningham into the bar.

"Well!" Trudy stood in the rear of the ABCO, hands on her hips. "A fine victory parade! Half a block!"

Alberta didn't look pleased either, but that was probably because nobody had stayed to help her down. The first time that had happened since she was thirteen.

"They practically ignored us," she said. "Just walked off and...."

"Trudence! Alberta!" Mrs. Philpot ran from the hotel, arms wide to embrace them. After the hugging and reassurances, she led Trudy and Alberta to the third floor. It was lovely to be fussed over, but Mrs. Philpot's questions were all about Quentin and the night they'd spent in Yuma. Quentin hadn't yet arrived by train to be questioned.

"He almost made us lose the race," Trudy told her, but her mother was more interested in the state of their reputations and health than in the race.

She insisted they lie down and rest before the gala. Bertha had soup, beds, drawn curtains and damp cloths for their foreheads. As she left them she said, "Guess all those shenanigans paid off. Didn't think you could do it but we're real proud you did."

The door closed before Trudy could thank her. She plunked down on the edge of the bed. "She's the only one! Everybody else treats us like so much extra baggage."

Alberta sat up. "The carpetbags! They're still in the ABCO!"

Mrs. Philpot sent a bellboy after them. He brought one. The other had been stolen.

"Yours!" wailed Alberta. "The one with the lotion!"

"Miss Peterson will mix us some more."

"But I need it *tonight!*"

"Your whole future depends on it, I suppose."

Alberta gave her an odd look, covered her eyes with the cloth and refused to say anything except, "I need my rest."

Trudy pulled back the curtains, but the windows looked onto the side of another building and the alley between was deserted. She sighed and lay down beside Alberta, hands clasped on her breast, and thought about justice and equality and the objectivity of the press and the unfairness of the Fates putting Alberta across the street from her when they knew John Baxter would come into their lives. As usual, her mother was right. She fell asleep.

Alberta shook her awake. "Look!"

On a table was a coffee service, the pot large enough to fill the two cups several times each. Trudy stared from it to Alberta.

"Bertha brought it," Alberta told her, "so we'll be bright-eyed for the gala. Come on! We have to get ready!"

Bertha (with help from Alberta, Trudy suspected) had done more than order coffee. Baths were being filled, the burner had been lit for the curling irons and the new clothes carefully spread on Alberta's side of the bed. Trudy's delight in the coffee was spoiled by the sight of her corset.

Madame Butashky was president of the San Julio Anti-Lacing Society. Every year she gave the Academy a talk on the dangers of tight corsets, complete with drawings of deformed rib cages. Trudy had insisted her gown be fitted to her natural body. But it had looked frumpy next to Alberta's until she'd let Alberta and the dressmaker coax her into trying a corset under it. She just wished she needn't feel guilty about looking her best.

They spent two hours primping and curling, pinning and lacing, biting their lips and pinching their cheeks. Bertha was in and out of the room "just to see how you're doing" but actually to keep an eye out for unladylike additions such as lip or cheek rouge. They did manage to dab talcum powder on their noses and liberally spot the inside of their gown hems with cologne. Alberta's had the heavy sweetness of "Nuit d'Amour."

"How did you manage that?" said Trudy.

"John Baxter bought it for me." Alberta smiled dreamily at her reflection in the mirror.

Before Trudy could answer, Mrs. Philpot swept into the room. "You look lovely!" She hugged them both carefully, then said, "Come now, your fathers are waiting."

Mr. Philpot and Mr. Cunningham looked stunned, then delighted to escort them. They offered their arms, Mr. Philpot giving one to Trudy and the other to his wife, and headed for the stairs. They could hear the roar of voices from the second floor. As they entered the ballroom, the band struck up "In My Merry Oldsmobile."

"There wasn't an Olds in the race," muttered Mr. Cunningham.

"Which is probably why they chose it," Mr. Philpot muttered back. "Safe and objective."

The crowd turned to see who'd entered, began to clap and draw back, leaving an aisle. Trudy started down it, grinning.

"Trudence," her mother whispered across Mr. Philpot.

Trudy tried to shift her grin to a modest smile but didn't quite succeed. She nodded at familiar faces, one of which belonged to Quentin. He looked tired but he was grinning, too. Stubby O'Dell was singing with three strangers, unheard over the band and applause. George Doty had a purple bruise on his left eye. With all the distractions, Trudy didn't see the ABCO until she was almost to the dais.

There it sat, dusty and battered, draped with garlands of bay laurel. The three-foot trophy rested on the driver's seat. On the other was propped a large sign: EASY AS ABC.

Trudy stopped, jerking her father sideways. The race officials were scattered through the crowd. The trophy had already been presented . . . to the ABCO.

"Magnificent," murmured Mr. Cunningham.

"I thought Alberta and I would get it," said Trudy.

"Why?" said Quentin. He and John Baxter came up to the red-carpeted dais.

"We won the race," Trudy told him. "Or didn't you hear?"

"The ABCO won the race. Anybody who drove it would have won."

"That isn't what you were saying two weeks ago!"

113

"Trudence!" There was no mistaking the warning in her mother's tone.

Trudy fumed inside, waiting for the band to begin the opening dance. She and Alberta would formally open the gala, Alberta dancing with her father, the owner of the ABCO. Trudy expected Quentin to be her partner, but it was John Baxter who stepped forward and swept her into the first waltz. They went twice around the room before Trudy recovered from her surprise. But not her anger. She wondered if John thought anybody could have won with the ABCO. She saw ex-Councilman Very talking earnestly to the newspaperman from Detroit. George Doty raised a glass in salute as Trudy whirled by.

"It's a pity my father couldn't be here instead of me," said John Baxter.

"Is he a newspaperman, too?" said Trudy.

"No, he produces ABCOs."

Trudy stumbled and stepped on his foot. She was still apologizing when Quentin cut in.

Through a tight smile and clenched teeth, she asked, "Why didn't you tell me?"

"You and Alberta had enough to worry about." He gave an impatient tug at her waist. "Will you pay attention?"

Their parents passed, smiling at them. Trudy wondered if her father had known. No, he would have printed it in the *Gazette*. The next turn showed her the ABCO and the trophy on its seat. Trudy smiled up at her brother and, on the next reverse, kicked him on the anklebone. Before she could kick the other one for

Alberta, Mr. Cunningham cut in. Her father claimed
the next dance and she was right, he hadn't known about
John.

"I'll have to telegraph Mathias Jr.," he said and
checked his pocket watch to see if the story would make
the next morning's *Gazette*.

Young men from Phoenix filled Trudy's dance program, but every time she began to enjoy herself, she
caught another look at the ABCO or John or her brother
and her anger flooded back. If Alberta hadn't signaled a
recess, Trudy would have.

The only secluded spot they could find was behind
the palm in the lobby and that stayed private only long
enough for Trudy to learn that John's father wanted
Trudy and Alberta to appear with the winning ABCO at
automobile shows in New York and Chicago.

"New York!" whispered Trudy.

But Alberta looked close to tears.

"I don't want to be an ABCO girl," she told Trudy.

Trudy stared at her. "Whyever not?"

"I don't want to leave Daddy or San Julio."

Trudy's heart sank. Mr. Baxter wouldn't want the
mechanician without the driver.

Half a dozen men came into the lobby. One was the
editor of the Phoenix *Examiner*. George Doty was telling
him how he'd rigged a Stillson wrench to substitute for a
lost hub.

"Then I notched the axle, see, and tied it . . . . Hey,
kiddos! Who are you hiding from?" He pointed at
Alberta. "That's the little lady gave me this shiner." He

didn't explain she'd just distracted him while he was cranking the Ford.

"It isn't the first time, either," he added. "You better steer clear of her, boys."

"He's drunk," Alberta whispered.

"Exhausted," whispered Trudy. The Ford had crossed the finish line less than an hour before. To George, Trudy said, "I'm glad you finally got here."

George pushed out his chest. "Not only got here, we came in third."

"You came in *last*," Trudy corrected. Gregory Sr. had missed the planks on the railroad bridge. After banging over the ties, the Model had been unable to continue. "Last," Trudy repeated.

George scowled, then started to grin and rock on his heels. "Well, we had to let you win. Ladies first or you cry your little eyes out."

Trudy took a step forward. "How would you like the other eye blackened?"

"Here you are!" John Baxter walked briskly up to the palm, smiling at Trudy and Alberta. "The buffet's ready." To George he said, "Glad you made it. That was a fine piece of repair work you did."

"Yeah, in spite of people sneaking up and yelling at me." George fingered his bruise gently, scowled and followed the others into the bar.

John said to Trudy, "I thought you were really going to hit him."

"I was. But my corset's too tight."

John looked startled, then laughed.

"Trudy!" said Alberta.

They strolled to the buffet room, John and Alberta making polite talk with people they met, Trudy brooding. The jab of whalebone stays had reminded her of Madame Butashky. Along with the niggling guilt had come the memory of Madame urging Trudy's mother to organize a Howdy Special for ladies. That was Madame's way, to organize. To *do*. If she were here . . . .

"They shouldn't try to serve gelatin in this weather."

Trudy blinked and found herself holding an empty plate and staring down at a molded fish with olive eyes and pimento scales.

"It's melting already," continued the plump woman at Trudy's side.

"Have you ever driven an automobile?" Trudy asked her.

The woman looked surprised. "Me?"

"Yes, you."

"No, never."

"Would you like to?"

"I couldn't." But she'd lost interest in the fake fish.

"Yes, you could. I'll show you." Trudy set her plate on the table, took the woman's filled one and set that down, too. "Come on."

"Ethel, Miriam," the woman called. "I'm going to have a driving lesson."

The woman's friends followed them into the nearly empty ballroom. Trudy stepped onto the dais.

"Ladies," she told them, "if you use gaslights, if you light the burner on your hot-water boiler, if you use a treadle sewing machine, you already know how to drive an ABCO."

There was an excited murmur. The three ladies increased to nine. Quentin, John and Alberta came to see where she'd gone, and as Trudy wove together the answers she'd given so often at the dealership, men as well as women gathered to hear.

"Just think what it means," Trudy finished. "No harnessing a smelly, shedding horse, no getting your skirts and boots dirty crossing streets. Just step into your ABCO, always ready at your doorstep, turn a lever and go! Easy as ABC!"

She grabbed the sign from the driver's seat, printed DEMONSTRATIONS on the back with the pencil attached to her dance program.

"Here!" She held up the sign. "Just sign here and tomorrow I will personally teach you to drive and care for your ABCO. Sign your name and tomorrow morning *you will drive this machine yourself!*"

John Baxter applauded silently, smiling that wonderful smile.

Trudy blushed.

Nineteen ladies signed for demonstrations.

"If one third buy ABCOs," Quentin figured, "or even a quarter of them . . . ."

"This is a stupendous idea," said John. "We should have you give ladies demonstrations at the automobile shows and maybe at ABCO dealerships. I must telegraph my father."

Alberta squeezed Trudy's hand.

"Sure you don't want to come, too?" whispered Trudy.

Alberta shook her head.

Trudy sighed. "I may not be going, either. There's still Mama."

But Mrs. Philpot agreed almost immediately, provided she and Bertha could accompany Trudy. That brought objections from Trudy's father.

"Nonsense," said Mrs. Philpot. "You can manage perfectly well with the Businessmen's Club and the hotel dining room."

"But this promoting could go on for years!" said Mr. Philpot.

"Perhaps. But if it does, I shall come home and leave Bertha to chaperone Trudence."

Trudy looked at Alberta and rolled her eyes.

"Of course," Mrs. Philpot continued, "if I find conditions unsuitable for a young lady, we will all be home immediately."

Trudy decided not to worry about that. She'd at least see Chicago, New York and Boston. Her mother certainly wouldn't go home until she'd had a visit with James. That had probably been a factor in her decision.

Trudy kept trying to persuade Alberta to change her mind. She couldn't imagine not having Alberta to talk over everything with. And she couldn't have managed the demonstrations without her.

Nineteen ladies had signed the card but twenty-seven came to the hotel. It took four days to give each of them a demonstration, though most were content with a ride around the block. Alberta alternated with Trudy, giving her time for fittings with the seamstress (most of her new wardrobe would be purchased in the east, the only thing Alberta envied), consultations with John about schedules and with her father about stories she could write for the *Gazette*. There were also letters of congratulations to answer.

Suzanne Davenport sent one, implying that one couldn't believe everything one read in the newspaper. Miss Dupree sent a telegram: MADAME BLANCHARD SAYS SOARING TO NEW HEIGHTS STOP CONGRATULATIONS AND FAIR WINDS ALOFT.

"Who's Madame Blanchard?" Trudy wondered.

John found out. She was a balloonist in France a hundred years before. It was the first time Trudy had known Miss Dupree to speak to a commoner on her psychophone.

Madame Butashky telephoned. It must have taken her most of the day to get lines clear all the way. Her voice kept fading and crackling but Trudy caught the gist of it. Congratulations on winning the race and admiration for thinking of giving free driving lessons.

"Brilliant strategem," shouted Madame. She sounded surprised that Trudy had thought of it, but that might have been only the whistling on the line ". . . wear bloomers . . . only sensible costume for automobiling . . . ." and her voice faded out for good.

Trudy hung up, her guilt gone. Women might not wear bloomers for automobiling but they certainly wouldn't be wearing corsets if they had to patch fuel lines or clean a burner. But until fashions changed, Trudy was wearing her corset under her new mauve traveling suit.

She felt very grown-up when Alberta drove them to the station. The ABCO was being shipped to San Julio on the same train with Alberta, her father, Mr. Philpot and Quentin.

The good-bys at the station were hurried. Quentin grumbled because she wasn't going back to San Julio to hold demonstrations for ladies. He held a list of ladies whose husbands had ordered ABCOs from the new Phoenix dealer, and most had received their demonstrations from Trudy.

"Alberta can give the demonstrations," Trudy told him. "After all, if an ABCO can win by itself, it can certainly sell itself, too."

She gave him a hug and a kiss. Her father had helped Bertha and Mrs. Philpot get settled. He stepped off the train. Trudy hugged and kissed him good-by, let the conductor help her aboard, then lifted her skirt and ran to where John had opened windows. She knelt on the seat and leaned out. Mrs. Philpot was busy waving to Quentin and Mr. Philpot from the other window.

Alberta walked alongside as the train began to pull out. "Write me all about it. Every day. Every single detail!"

"You can come, too. Just for a while and go home with Mama."

But she'd said it all a dozen times and Alberta's answer was still the same.

"I don't want to leave Daddy or San Julio."

"Or Fred Auklander."

"Fred Auklander?" Alberta was trotting now, but she managed a wide-eyed look that made Trudy want to stay and worm the cause out of her. "Why would I want to stay with Fred Auklander?"

She stopped and waved as the train pulled away. After a glance to see that John Baxter was really on the seat beside her, Trudy waved back.

The horsewoman and the bicyclist must take a back seat. The ABCO Girl has come to town. Trim as a filly running on grass . . . .

New York HERALD, *October 14, 1910*

. . . an ethereal vision in satin and French lace. The Maid of Honor was the groom's sister, Miss Trudence Philpot, taking a brief respite before her lecture tour takes her to England and La Belle France. It will be remembered that the bride was also an ABCO girl and her betrothal crowned her winning of the Great Mountain to Desert Race. . . .

Miss Dupree, San Julio GAZETTE, *June 20, 1911*

THE FACTS

This book is based on accounts of a real Great Desert Race that was run between Los Angeles and Phoenix each fall from 1908 to 1914. The course of the race, which varied from year to year, often followed most of the route described here. The first race, in 1908, was won by a White Steamer, but no female automobilists competed.

In the early years of the century, steam-powered automobiles were more common than gasoline cars, and there were many different makes and models. Everything said about steam cars here is true, though not necessarily true for every make. The ABCO is a composite of several, primarily the Stanley Steamer and the White.

No steam car was ever mass-produced. Gasoline cars gained in popularity once a dependable self-starter was developed, and the last Stanley Steamer was made in 1925. Steamers were cheap and simple to operate, silent and non-polluting. If someone would make them again, I'd be first in line to buy one.

—Betty Baker

About the Author

BETTY BAKER has written outstanding books for children of all ages. Her books for younger readers include *Latki and the Lightning Lizard* (an IRA-CBC "Children's Choice for 1980"), *Three Fools and a Horse* (a Child Study Association "Book of the Year 1975") and *At the Center of the World* (a School Library Journal "Best Book of 1973"). Among her books for older readers are *Save Sirrushany!*, *The Spirit Is Willing* (a Child Study Association "Book of the Year 1974" and "Kirkus Choice Book") and *A Stranger and Afraid* (a *New York Times* "Outstanding Children's Book of 1972").

Her *Settlers and Strangers* was a Non-Fiction Honor Book in the 1978 Boston Globe-Horn Book Awards, and *The Dunderhead War* won the 1967 Spur Award. She has won the Western Heritage Award for the Outstanding Western juvenile book twice: in 1963 for *Killer-of-Death*, and in 1970 for *And One Was a Wooden Indian*.

Ms. Baker has lived for a number of years in the Southwest, which she has used as background for many of her books.